THE RILEY BROTHERS BOOK 3

E. DAVIES

Publisher's Note: This is a work of fiction. Names, characters, places, and incidents are a product of the author's imagination. Locales and public names are sometimes used for atmospheric purposes. Any resemblance to actual people, living or dead, or to businesses, companies, events, institutions, or locales is completely coincidental.

Swish / E. Davies. – 2nd ed.
ISBN: 978-1-912245-02-4

CHAPTER

One

THOMAS

"How's your hand?"

"I'll be fine," Cam laughed, the sound carrying through the cold winter morning. "It won't fall off from shoveling the driveway once. Let me do this."

Thomas glanced across his windshield to Cameron's driveway. His arms burned from scraping the ice off in quick, sharp thrusts of plastic across glass. It was the hard kind of ice; shard-like ice chunks sprayed across his hands and face.

God, January mornings were the worst. The sun wasn't even up yet, but he was already out and cleaning up the driveway with his brothers and their boyfriends. Now that Noah lived with Cam and Chase with Jackson, they had five people to help. Good thing since last night's freezing rain and snow had left a mess.

Sometimes only one or two of them got up early. They tried to shovel at least each other's walkways if they had time before work. Other times, Thomas barely had time to dig himself out of the snow, but when he came home from work his driveway was cleared.

It was nice to be able to count on his neighbors to swap favors. Living between his brothers had its perks, even if he wanted to knock their heads together sometimes.

With all the extra hours he was taking lately, helping cover shifts thanks to his coworker Cassandra's winter trip to the Caribbean, he was gone even more. Then again, he had a forty-hour work week as it was. He knew he was damned lucky.

"Getting cold?" Thomas called across the thin row of branches. In the summer, it was a leafy hedge separating their driveways.

Noah, the now live-in boyfriend of one of his big brothers, had already pulled off Cam's glove. He was rubbing Cam's right hand briskly to warm it up again. Ever since his denervation surgery, Cam had said half of his body reacted differently to the cold. But that was a small price to pay for a decreased risk of heart failure.

"No, I'm fine." Cam swatted Noah lightly and laughed. "I'll go inside if I'm in danger of frostbite." He pulled on his glove and briskly shoveled again, clearing a path down to the mailbox and street.

Noah still stayed nearby and eyed him suspiciously as he cleaned up after Cameron. He hadn't let Cam shovel alone over the last two weeks. Just before Christmas, Cam had been declared safe to occasionally exercise, but they still hadn't let him.

"What's wrong?"

Jackson was the oldest of the three brothers, and he lived on the other side of Thomas. He was leaning on his shovel and peering over the scraggly hedge at Thomas, then beyond at Cam. No doubt he was concerned that Cam was having an episode of some kind for the first time since surgery. Behind him, Jackson's boyfriend, Chase, was watching.

"No, it's fine," Thomas assured them both with a laugh. "Just his one cold hand."

"I've heard of special gloves that can warm your hands up," Chase spoke up. He pulled down the back gate of Jackson's truck to shovel the bed out. "I should've gotten you those for Christmas."

"Or a plane ticket to Florida," Cam suggested. "I'll accept that."

"Excuse me?" Noah pulled the rim of Cam's toque down over his eyes.

Cam laughed and yanked it back up again. "Two plane tickets," Cam corrected himself, grinning at his boyfriend.

Thomas's heart squeezed a little as he watched the two interact. Cam and Noah had been dating since April. They met when Cam and Thomas joined Jackson in their hometown of Fredericton. The two men were still going strong, and he admired the deep affection they both held for each other.

Jackson and Chase had only been dating since about August – exactly when wasn't really clear. Neither would say exactly when it had turned from friendship to romance. They were just as sweet as Cam and Noah.

That left just Thomas single. By choice as much as by chance, really. It wasn't like he hadn't had offers...

Ugh. Thomas pushed that thought aside and kept scraping the windshield, cleaning off the last few bits of ice. He pushed the wipers back down with twin muffled thumps and scraped the rest of the windows.

At last, Thomas shoveled a path for his car down to the

street. It was gonna be a little hairy until he got to the well-plowed streets beyond suburbia, but he'd grown up driving here. He knew as well as his brothers how to avoid losing all control.

In every area of his life, too. Sometimes, though he'd never admit it, he *wanted* someone to sweep into his life. He wanted to be unable to turn down a good thing. Noah had entered Cam's life with a bang, and Chase had started a whirlwind romance with Jackson.

Could he have something like that?

Thomas dropped off his shovel on the porch and grabbed his lunch from inside, then locked up his house. "See you guys later," he waved to a chorus of goodbyes as he climbed into his car and started it up. The engine turned over a few extra times. Then, it purred to life and he was gliding through the drifts for the short, chilly drive to the bank.

CHAPTER
Two

ALEX

THE ROCK MUSIC COMING THROUGH THE SPEAKERS IN THE CAR was so soft it was almost inaudible. Alex leaned back in the driver's seat, his profile half-hidden to passersby. Not that anyone was walking down the quiet street this time of night. It was the perfect location, and Alex ought to have been glad.

Instead, Alex was more restless than usual. He'd spent hundreds of hours, going on thousands by now, just sitting on stakeouts. This time, he got to sit in the car and listen to music. He even checked his phone when he dared to take his eyes off the front of the house. Compared to some of his previous cases in Ontario, and here in New Brunswick, this was a cakewalk.

"Must be the caffeine," he murmured to himself at last, rubbing his eyes. He focused on a few points, in the distance and close to him, to keep them fresh. He'd grabbed a coffee from Tim's before coming out here, expecting he might have to stay up late.

Alex much preferred the kind of surveillance that ended around three or four in the afternoon. He'd be home and relaxing in front of the TV before most people were even finished work.

But cheaters weren't always caught at noon. This one favored late nights, even though his wife was staying with a friend for the week.

This would be a lot easier if he could just go back to his old ways. Alex had been a *fantastic* honey trap, even for straight men like this Darren seemed to be. But he'd had to knock that off since moving back here. Plus, with a gay community this small, he might wind up working for women who'd married gay men. That came with too much baggage even for him.

Movement.

He froze, and then slowly raised his camera to rest on the windowsill. He hit the record button and zoomed in until he got a good look at the woman stepping out of the house. As far as he knew, the house didn't belong to either the cheater or the mistress, Anna. It was owned by one of Darren's buddies. That guy had to be in on it, or else the cheating asshole Darren was good at keeping it quiet.

Darren's wife, Lexy, had hired him to find out for sure if Darren was cheating, and if so, with whom. She especially wanted to know if it was an ongoing affair or a one-time mistake. A series of one-time mistakes seemed better to her than an affair.

Alex had wanted to tell her that it didn't matter. An asshole cheating on her with a string of women was no better than with one woman. He knew a lot of people didn't think that way. Back in his honey trap days... well, Christ, he was glad to say goodbye to some aspects of that job.

The problem, of course, was that he had no other choice *than* to say goodbye to his Ontario jobs. He'd been forced to move back here, and now he had to take whatever cases he was offered. Things were getting a little better though. Lexy had gotten his name as a reference from a friend he'd worked with. Referrals meant steady business.

But still... there was no plan B.

Anna stepped into her car and waved, then pulled out of the driveway as Darren leaned in the doorway. Darren disappeared back inside and, within a minute, was back out and heading to his car. It was nothing to tail him back to his apartment building. Alex sat outside just long enough to make sure the lights were off and Darren had gone to bed, then rubbed his face.

That was it for the night. Hours of waiting and watching for one little clip in the 1 a.m. darkness. They hadn't even kissed goodbye.

"That's okay," Alex muttered. "I'll catch you sooner or later, asshole."

Alex pulled away again. He wanted rotisserie chicken and chips from the 24-hour grocery store nearby. He'd eat and watch TV by himself – as always – and get some sleep.

It was a far cry from his last life, where he might have gone to a club or picked a number from his phone after eating and showering. But he had a reputation to keep here.

"Rep, shmep," he muttered, but it was a peaceful protest. On some level, Alex appreciated a quieter routine in his sleepy, small hometown. The quiet hours watching people together just drove home the less-balanced aspects of his life.

And when he thought too hard about it, half his reluctance to go out and socialize was unsurprising. He'd had a steady downhill slide in his mood since... oh, November. Maybe it was SAD; maybe he was just depressed about being stuck here. No longer was he making bank and sleeping with hot guys every other weekend.

He'd had friends, but he'd drifted out of touch with them over the summer. Working his ass off, taking every job he got, kept him too busy. A lot of people just didn't get his life – irregular schedules, confidentiality agreements, occasional danger... And then there was incredible monotony.

For once, he didn't let himself mope as he crawled into bed. When one guy turned him down, another might be around the corner. Sometime, he'd find what he'd been missing for years. Maybe not in exactly the same form, but... something close.

CHAPTER

Three

THOMAS

"I can help the next--"

Thomas would know that face anywhere. Scruffy dark stubble, piercing bright eyes, pink lips curved up in a knowing little smile...

"--person here," Thomas finished with determination. He ripped his gaze from the man at the back of the line to the front.

As the client stepped up to his window, Thomas took his debit card and the check he wanted to deposit. He moved on autopilot, as it took every ounce of determination he had not to stare at Alex.

Alex: his ex, the man who'd loved him and run. The man who'd bumped into him one day and got his number somehow. They'd texted, hot and cold, and then Thomas had gone cold. Finally, Alex had shown up at his house late one night. Thomas had *finally* said yes to his repeated pleas to see him. Alex had tried to apologize...

Thomas didn't like to think of himself as bitter, but he also thought he had perfectly good reason to be. Alex had fucked up both his brothers' lives. He'd spied on Cam and Chase, nearly putting Jackson in harm's way too.

But he still remembered the way Alex's face had fallen that late August evening. Alex had so passionately explained how he hadn't *meant* to harm them. He'd been hired to find out Cam's disability status and Chase's location. He had to take the jobs. Thomas had reminded him that the end result was the same.

And besides, he hadn't forgiven Alex for fucking running out on him *before*. That was back when Alex was eighteen and Thomas was sixteen. Love then was getting a ride home from Alex after classes and feeling each other up in the south Fredericton parks.

Fuck.

Thomas cleared his throat. "The funds will be processed and available within five business days. Can I help you with anything else?"

"No, thanks," the client answered, taking back his card and leaving with a quick goodbye.

Alex was three from the front.

The next customer wanted the limit raised on his debit card. That was a quick job, but Thomas refused to rush through it. He wasn't going to try to get Alex, or to avoid serving him. He was going to proceed at the same damn pace he always did.

Thomas's throat went dry, and his, "Have a good day..." almost died on his lips. The client walked off and he looked up for the next one.

Alex was at the front of the line.

Before he invited him up, Alex was crossing the smooth tile floor, striding toward him. His winter jacket was unzipped. Thomas's gaze crawled briefly up the leather jacket underneath. Alex wore dark jeans and a collared shirt that hugged the smooth skin of his neck...

He hadn't seen Alex since he'd sent him home that night in August after the barbecue. Alex had tried to flirt with him and Thomas had... crushed him. Thomas had never specifically said he *didn't* want a date. He'd just told him flat-out that he had a lot to deal with without Alex trying to charm the pants off him.

Thomas hoped his voice was steady. "How can I help you?"

That smile was back. Alex's slow smile, the way his eyes crinkled in the corners and his teeth glinted... Thomas had loved that smile from the first time he saw it.

"Nice to see you again, Thomas." Alex folded his arms and leaned on the counter, closing the scarce space between them. It was like electric jolts jumped between them, even though a good foot still separated them.

Thomas's heart raced and he kept his grip on his mouse firm as his skin tingled. "You, too." Alex's eyes were locked on his, and his lips were slightly parted as he drew a breath. Thomas resisted the urge to stare at his lips, as much as he wanted to. Those lips had once known where exactly on his neck would make him hard in seconds.

Did Alex still remember those spots? Was he even better now?

Alex's eyes dragged down from Thomas's eyes to his lips, then his neck. Thomas's chest pounded as he tried to dismiss those ideas. He resisted the urge to tug his collar up or flatten his tie and just glanced at his computer, then back at Alex. "Can I help you?"

Alex was looking him in the eye again, squarely enough that it almost made Thomas wonder if he'd indulged in fantasy instead of observation. But no, there was no imagining the glint behind Alex's eyes when he saw something he wanted.

Every damn time he bumped into Alex, there it was again. And it always felt like they'd split up just a week ago, maybe a month ago – not years ago. The chemistry between them was still as raw and passionate as if they were waiting to fall into bed at any moment.

"I need to make an appointment to discuss mortgages."

Thomas's eyebrows rose. The young man who'd run to Ontario just as Thomas had been considering taking the biggest leap of all with him? *Now* he was getting a mortgage? "On a local property?"

Alex didn't miss the implication. His brows drew together slightly. Then the look disappeared, replaced by an ironic little smile... maybe even self-deprecating. "Yes. I'm settling down and looking for a house. But the appointment has to be next Thursday at two PM. My schedule is... quite busy."

"Well, the service desk is over there," Thomas said as politely as possible. Someone else was in charge of that, and he had the oddest feeling Alex had known that. Alex had just wanted to see him and maybe... tempt him. Christ, and it worked every time. Thomas licked his lips and straightened up. "Maggie can help you book an appointment at a convenient time."

"Thank you," Alex murmured, then straightened up again.

"Is there anything else I can help you with?" Thomas narrowed his eyes slightly in warning. The Alex he knew would make a lewd comment, and now was hardly the time or place.

Alex's eyes crinkled as that self-assured little smirk

curved his lips. Then, Alex shook his head. "No, thanks. Have a good day."

Thomas was left watching his retreating back as Alex walked toward the service desk to make his appointment. He pulled himself back together and looked for the next customer.

No matter what Alex thought, he wasn't lying around and moping, waiting to fall into his arms or bed. Of all the people Alex had known or dated, Thomas hadn't heard of anyone more resistant than him. Not just because Thomas liked playing hard-to-get, but because... that was the way he was.

And, as ever, that seemed to be exactly what pulled Alex to him like a moth to a porch light. What pulled Thomas to Alex in return? Everything about him, whether Thomas liked it or not.

Thomas pushed him out of mind to focus on his clients' needs. He couldn't be distracted at work – not while he was angling for a promotion.

He needed this. He was definitely the lowest-paid of the three of them, even though Cam had seasonal work and Jackson was practically a freelancer. Tellers didn't earn a fortune, and he had house renovations to pay off.

Work was his future; love was a fleeting fancy, so work came first. And work *definitely* came before exes and enemies. And both, in one sexy, smoldering, self-assured package of hunk that Thomas wanted *so* badly to hate.

CHAPTER
Four

ALEX

Fuck, Thomas was *hot*.

Since he did his banking online, Alex hadn't had a chance to run into Thomas since August. But Thomas was hotter than ever. He was clearly sorting out conflicting emotions: anger and attraction. Oh, yeah. Alex had seen the way Thomas shifted...

And there was always that unspoken thread between them.

They missed each other, on some level or another. Maybe most exes did. Alex hadn't stuck around any of his other exes long enough to find out. He'd ditched one and gone straight to another, cutting exes out of his life with surgical precision. Impossible to do that here, even if he'd wanted to. The town was too small. Thomas, of course, worked at Alex's goddamn bank and he wasn't about to switch banks to avoid his ex. That was a low he refused to stoop to.

Really, Alex *didn't* want to cut Thomas out. He'd wanted more. A date, maybe, to get to know each other again after all these years.

Alex had known Thomas moved back to town about a month after he had. He'd sent a few texts, but they'd never really gone anywhere. Just casual brushoffs from Thomas. So he'd kept his distance at first before going to the Rileys' neighborhood barbecue last summer. He'd had to tell Chase that his asshole family was gone for good... and of course, Thomas had been right there.

They'd swapped words and Thomas had invited him over that night. Just as Alex thought he might get lucky, Thomas put down his foot and told him not to keep asking him out. Alex respected that, much as he disliked it.

Thomas had never actually said he didn't *want* to see him again, though. He'd said Cam was sick, Jackson and Chase needed renovation help, his family had lots on the go, work was busy...

Not that he didn't *want* a date.

Alex had let him get away with it, but it still bugged him.

He got to the front of the short line in front of the service desk. Right. The appointment.

"Hello," he greeted, turning on his usual charming smile. "I wondered if you'd help me arrange an appointment to discuss mortgages. I have a rough work schedule, though. I'm really only available around 2 p.m. next Thursday. I'm sorry for being difficult."

"Oh, not at all, love. That's fine. I'll see what I have for that time."

Warming people up with an apology worked a charm here in Atlantic Canada. He'd missed that.

"Well, the closest I have is two-thirty... would that be fine, Mr. Walker?"

Score. He'd just turn up early for his appointment. "That's

okay," he assured this receptionist – Maggie – with another bright smile. "Who's the appointment with?"

"Lisa, one of our senior loan officers."

"Thank you. Excellent." Lisa's office was next to Anna's. He might get a glimpse into Anna's office on the way past. He'd have to bring a hidden camera... maybe the phone in the shirt front pocket trick.

The next step was to watch Anna for the next day or two. Darren might be visiting her. He'd do that once she left work – for now, he had enough time to grab lunch.

He took the card with the appointment time and wished Maggie a good day. On the way past the tellers' desks, Alex let his gaze sweep across the empty lineup and desks. Lunchtime over with, the rush to get to the bank had subsided.

He wasn't surprised to see Thomas watching him. Thomas tore his gaze away and looked at the computer, but he was blushing.

Alex smiled again as he pushed open the heavy bank door and stepped onto the icy sidewalk. As he walked out, he felt Thomas's eyes on him. A glance through the window confirmed it; he was looking at him again. Alex winked to let him know he'd seen him before walking off.

For the first time in days, his heart was light despite the gray skies.

He might win Thomas over yet.

Five

THOMAS

"I'm fine with pasta."

"Are you sure?" Thomas poured a little more white wine into the pan and stirred the chicken and vegetables again. He glanced over at Noah, who sprawled on a stool at the breakfast bar. Noah's elbow was propped on the counter, chin on his fist.

"Quite sure," Noah chuckled. "Carb-loading to make up for shoveling snow. I hope the winter's not going to be that bad. Early mornings are the worst."

Thomas grabbed a box of cream from the fridge. "Only another few months. But yeah... going to the bank before it's light and coming home after it's dark when I work such an easy job..."

"Mmhmm. And the days are getting longer." Noah twirled a lock of his hair.

"Exactly." Thomas shut the fridge and poured cream into the pan, then added some flour to make a creamy sauce. The pasta water boiled, so he dumped the noodles in.

Noah perked up a little. "How's your work thing coming along?"

Thomas tensed up, the stress ball knotting his chest. "I'm helping everywhere I can. Irma needed help with a late client yesterday and I did that. Uh, I'm kind of helping Maggie out when she's not at her desk. I'm trying to show initiative."

"You think they're hiring soon?"

No. Thomas sighed. "I... don't know. At the very least, I can get a good performance review. Or a good reference if I switch to another bank that *does* need senior positions filled."

"How desperate are you?" Noah asked. "Are you talking sometime down the road, or now?"

Thomas winced. He wasn't running out of money – his job covered the bills, after all – but with the extra money on the mortgage from renovations, his savings were gone. He wasn't earning quite enough to replenish them. And unlike Cam, who split bills with Noah, and Jackson, who had Chase to help out, he was a single-income household. "Sooner the better."

"You can always do casual work--"

"No, no," Thomas chuckled lightly, trying to brush it off. "So, enough about me... you think you've got SAD for sure?"

"I'm almost sure of it," Noah sighed, easily distracted. "I've got one of those light lamps from Costco though."

"Oh yeah?" Thomas stirred the pan as the sauce thickened. "Is it helping?"

Noah nodded. "A little. Being around Cam all the time helps. It's not much fun having to go to work more than him."

Since surgery, Cam hadn't gone to work. As an apprentice beekeeper, it was the down season anyway. There wasn't much Cam's boss, Noah's uncle, and Cam could do in the middle of the winter. Of course, Noah still had to go to the gallery where he worked as an art curator.

"That must be hard," Thomas nodded. "Cam's resting up, though, huh? How's he doing?"

"He's hoping to lower his beta blocker dose in the next month or two. When he gets back to Toronto for the next follow-up, they're gonna see if it's safe." Noah fidgeted with his hair, then picked up his beer bottle for a swig. "So far, he hasn't fainted at all or even felt dizzy."

"Since surgery? And it's been a month now," Thomas marveled. "That must be awesome."

"It's incredible! We're hoping he won't have to get an ICD." That brought a smile to Noah's face. "And he's been exercising since then, too. And we've been testing things out, too, you know..."

Thomas laughed and cut Noah off. "Okay, I'm glad, but I'm fine without knowing more."

"Yeah," Noah grinned. "Still only a couple times a week, but--"

"That's plenty enough," Thomas snorted, shutting off the stove. He dumped the pasta into a strainer, then back into the pot. Once he added the sauce and stirred it together, he looked at Noah when there wasn't an answer. Noah was watching him with a raised eyebrow. "What? It is, for most people..."

"Yeah, but we missed half our honeymoon phase."

Thomas winced. Cam hadn't even been properly diagnosed when they'd met. Cam had had to travel back to Ontario to see real experts. When they'd figured it out, he'd been instantly banned from exercise and his sex life had been... rather limited. Most new couples *did* have the most active sex life in those first few months of living together.

Or so popular myths said. Thomas didn't know from personal experience.

"Sorry," Thomas told him. "I didn't think about that."

Noah shook his head, forgiving the mistake. "It's fine. I'm just glad things feel more... normal now."

Thomas nodded, ladling pasta into two bowls. "I should probably get laid now and then, too," he smiled. "I don't know what's normal." It was still bizarre talking about his love life with anyone even remotely connected to his family. He was trying.

"Mm? I can go out to the bar with you," Noah offered, grinning. "Or Chase. You know he's up for a gay club... *the* gay club." There was only one in town, after all. His eyes narrowed as he watched Thomas's reactions.

Thomas shook his head, not giving Noah anything to work with. Those weren't his scenes at all. Besides...

"There's someone else who's been on my mind. I just don't know if it's a good idea," Thomas admitted, carrying the bowls over to the table.

Noah slid off the stool and sashayed over. "Ohhh? You've never mentioned someone before." His eyes gleamed with mischief. "Who is this person?"

"It's... it's a long story," Thomas laughed. "But I've been kind of avoiding them since... oh, August..."

"*August?*" Noah dropped his fork in his bowl. "Jesus, Thomas, it's January! Did you ghost them?"

"Ghost them?" Thomas didn't know that term.

"Go offline, you know – block them or stop responding after a good date, with no explanation. Just vanish."

Thomas shook his head. "Not exactly." He nibbled his lip, then dipped his fork into the pasta. "Bon appetit."

"Merci," Noah winked. "But, man, it's already mid-winter.

If you're still thinking about them..." He counted quickly on his fingers. "Four, five months later...?"

Months? Try four or five years! "I know. It's stupid," Thomas laughed. "But... maybe I'll try a date."

"They're still interested in you?"

Oh, definitely. With the way Alex had looked him over at the bank... then winked at him on the way out... Alex was still interested.

He was just waiting for Thomas to say the word. And he knew Alex was going to come into the bank next Thursday...

Or maybe he shouldn't be looking to get over Alex by seeing him again. Maybe he should be looking for someone else. He had an online dating profile that he checked every week or two. He'd never had more than one or two dates with any guy he'd met through it. If he thought too hard about it, Thomas knew he'd always subconsciously compared them to Alex.

Maybe he'd have another look, though.

Once Noah was back with Cam and Thomas was alone in his house, he started up his laptop and navigated again to the dating site. He sprawled on the couch, the laptop on his stomach as he squinted at the screen. He awkwardly typed in the password, the screen rising and falling as he waited for it to load.

A few new messages, but none of them were interesting. One was from a student. Technically, the guy was his own age, but Thomas was out of school and in a different stage of life. It just felt weird to date students. A couple were for hookups and not with anyone really appealing. Now and then, he added *casual sex* to the list of things he was looking for, but only once every few months, when his urges got too strong.

There wasn't an easy way to say he only wanted to date men if they were a lot like... fucking Alex.

"For fuck's sake." Thomas closed his laptop and dug out his phone, pressing it to his forehead for a second. He half-hoped Siri would whisper to him that this was a bad idea.

With no enlightenment coming from the gadget, he unlocked it and opened a new text message. He added Alex's number.

Good seeing you. Want to hang out?

Thomas hesitated for a long minute, debating if he should add something: *I'm still annoyed at you.* Or worse yet, *Do you miss me?* He pressed "send" before he took back the decision. Then, he shoved the phone under himself and rubbed his face with a groan.

He didn't trust himself to be alone with Alex. No matter how much some things about Alex annoyed him, his apology had been sincere. And as much as he hated that Alex had left him to train for his career in the big city and probably fuck guys who were *properly* gay, that had also been years ago.

And they'd never fucked. As high school boyfriends, Thomas had always said no. He hadn't been ready for it. Unlike all his shitty peers, he'd never had a problem saying no and meaning it. And Alex had never pushed him hard. He'd coaxed now and then, but when it was clear that Thomas just wasn't into it, Alex had gracefully accepted that.

Of course, Thomas had fucked other men later, when he was ready to admit he wanted it. But he'd never loved a man as deeply as Alex, and the two of them had never gone that far. Maybe the key to getting over Alex was doing it for the first time.

It was logical enough, on the surface. At least it was a great excuse for falling into bed with his first boyfriend and now least favorite person.

And this opened up the lines of communication again. It was the first time since he'd invited Alex over in August to tell him – in less abrasive terms – to fuck off. Alex had respected his wishes. It was scary to think how much he'd *wanted* Alex to call him, just out of the blue.

This was the permission he sensed Alex had been waiting for.

"Enough bullshit thinking," Thomas muttered, hauling himself to his feet. He'd clean the living room, just in case Alex did come over. And if Alex wasn't interested, he'd still have a clean living room. He refused to admit that he was listening over the vacuum cleaner's hum for the chime of his cell phone.

ALEX'S PHONE VIBRATED IN HIS POCKET. HE DIDN'T DRAG HIS eyes off the house for a moment. He fumbled for his phone, swiping his fingers down the screen to get it to read out the text.

Text message today at 8:02 PM. Thomas.

Good seeing you. Want to hang out?

The phone's voice was about the least sexy thing imaginable. It made Alex grin nonetheless. "Fuck, yeah," he whispered.

He squinted through the living room window as he pressed the speech button and dictated. "Would love to see you, period. When and where, question mark." Then, he pressed send.

Seconds later, he had an answer read out in the same rapid robotic voice. He really needed to change it to some sexy man, at least.

Text message today at 8:05 PM. Thomas.

Tonight.

"Oh, yeah," Alex smirked. He leaned back in his seat

again, raising his camera when he saw motion. It was only a brief flicker, though, so he frowned and lowered it again.

Since Darren had walked into Anna's house two hours ago, there had been no sign of activity. More importantly, the living room drapes were open. If they weren't socializing in the living room like platonic friends...

Heh, and Thomas wasn't texting to socialize. He'd cracked that facade with his visit to the bank, he was certain of it. The only question was: did Thomas just want to hook up, or did he want more afterward? Was this flame rekindling, and if so, did Thomas like that idea as much as he did?

He dictated, "I'm working until late, comma, probably past your bedtime, period. Still OK, question mark?" It came easily to him to dictate texts now when he couldn't take his eyes off the stakeout. It had taken weeks of practice to get used to it, though.

Text message today at 8:09 PM. Thomas.

That's fine. Come over to my house when you're done with work.

Alex smirked and dictated, "Great, period. See you soon, period." He folded his hands behind his head and stretched out. God, he hoped Darren was going to have an early night.

***

Alex got his wish: around nine-thirty, there was a stir of motion in the window. He pressed *record*, then rolled down his window and watched closely.

The microphone was aimed in just the right spot. After a few seconds of wind crackling, he picked up on sound.

"--at the cross-country ski cabin?"

Anna's voice was unmistakable after having tracked her

for days. "The main cabin? Yeah, at noon?"

Darren murmured his agreement. "Noon's great. We'll figure out the details on Thursday..."

"Shh," Anna giggled. Alex rolled his eyes but listened and watched closely. They were standing a bit too close, but there was no physical contact. No real evidence yet.

But he was positive that Lexy's suspicions had been right. And now he knew when and where to get the video his client and Darren's wife, Lexy, wanted.

"I'll see you alone, right?"

"Of course. I'll feign a headache and keep the lights dim and the blinds closed..." Anna's voice was soft now, almost inaudible as she sidled flirtatiously. Then, she shooed him with her hands. "Go on, you better get home before the roads get bad."

Darren waved. "I'll see you Thursday afternoon, Ms. Forester. I sure hope we can work out some favorable terms..."

He was stepping into his car now and Anna laughed as she went inside, shaking her head. Alex held his breath, but Darren didn't look around. He just started up and carefully pulled out onto the street.

After shutting off the camera and microphone, Alex cracked his knuckles.

It was a good thing they were cross-country skiing, not downhill. Alex could do cross-country. He'd break his neck trying to follow them downhill.

God, this job was made for him. Alex let his ego swell warmly in his chest. He waited a few minutes, then started up the car to drive toward Thomas's house. Snowflakes fell thickly on his windshield, but snow or no snow, he had an appointment to keep.

CHAPTER
Seven

THOMAS

Thomas wasn't even twenty-two years old yet. Ten o'clock ought to have been early to him, he knew. But he'd never been the type to go out clubbing until all hours. Neither did he like to wake up early. He usually went to bed around ten and read for a few hours before falling asleep.

Still being up and dressed at ten, pacing around the living room and tidying up, was downright weird. Knowing he was waiting for Alex, who could blow through right now or at 3 a.m., was even worse.

From nine onward, every time he heard a purring engine on the street, Thomas peeked through the blinds. He knew it was too early since Alex said he'd be up late, but he couldn't help himself.

It was a surprise when he pushed aside the blind and a familiar dark car was parked at the bottom of his driveway. The driver's side car door opened.

Oh, Jesus. Here he comes.

Thomas refused to wait by the door. He sat on the couch, aware of his hands in his lap, his heart pounding in his chest.

He *felt* Alex's approach up the walkway to his porch and his door...

For a moment, it felt like Thomas was being stalked by a predator he'd invited home. It didn't scare him – it thrilled him.

The doorbell rang and the moment of tension was gone. He stood up, briskly heading for the door and opening it.

Sure enough, Alex leaned on his door frame, all muscles and confident smile. His hair was messy and stuck up on the back, his thumb in his jacket pocket.

Christ, he was so fucking hot.

Thomas pushed open the screen door until Alex moved, then stepped inside to let him in. "Hello."

"Hey there," Alex answered. Thomas almost wished he'd wipe that arrogant little smirk off his face, but it looked too damn hot. "I got off early."

"I trust that doesn't happen often."

Alex paused, his smirk growing into a grin as they both registered the innuendo of the moment. Thomas's cheeks heated up, but he refused to take back the words. "No. Not often."

"Come on in."

Alex left his jacket and shoes in the foyer and Thomas led him into the house. "Want a drink of water or anything?"

"No thanks. I'm good."

They moved together for the couch. For a moment, as Alex and Thomas sank down together and turned toward each other, it felt like old days. It was like they were about to grab PlayStation controllers or a DVD to watch together...

Thomas swallowed hard and caught Alex's gaze. "I'm still angry at you for taking the job for Cam, knowing he was my brother. And about what happened when we broke up," he told him plainly. "But I haven't been able to get you out of my head. Seeing you at the bank... God, it felt like no time had passed since August."

"When you threw me out?" Alex quipped, his lips drawing up from a serious listening face to a teasing one instead. "I knew you shouldn't have. I knew we still had chemistry."

Thomas glared at Alex. He couldn't deny it: having Alex sitting so close their knees bumped made a jolt of pleasure run through him. The electric chills reminded him of everything they'd had together – and what they hadn't.

"So this isn't a first date... or first-date-since... well, you know." Alex trailed off and laughed. "This is a booty call."

"That's not--" Thomas cut himself off. Okay, maybe it was a little accurate.

Fuck, he wasn't the kind of guy to have hate sex with his ex. This wasn't about being angry. And he'd slept with strangers before, in his experimenting days in Halifax.

Why did this feel so different?

"Maybe," Thomas corrected himself, his voice tight as he clenched his jaw. He dug his fingers into the back of the couch behind Alex's head, touching his hair with his other hand. "That's probably the best description."

Alex's fingertips on the back of his hand were surprisingly gentle. "I won't tell a soul," he murmured, drawing Thomas's gaze back to his own.

God, those beautiful, long-lashed eyes. He lost himself in those eyes for a moment. He *wanted* to lose himself even further...

Alex's hand ran up his arm toward his shoulder and the last of Thomas's resistance melted away. The pleasurable tingles at being touched by familiar, skillful hands overwhelmed him. Even more chills of pleasure reverberated down his spine.

Thomas's breath caught as Alex slid closer so their thighs pressed together. He turned sideways and hooked his ankle around Thomas's as if he were about to roll over and straddle him. First, though, Alex took the time to touch the back of Thomas's neck. Alex played with the short hairs there as he looked him up and down.

"You got hotter."

Thomas blushed. "You were always hot," he murmured. Alex had only been a couple years older, but by god, he'd looked twenty before he was even out of school. That was probably how he'd gotten hired in security right out of high school.

Right when Thomas had been ready to say *yes* to everything Alex meant.

He swallowed back the memory. Strangely, it wasn't hard to do so. The moment was melancholic, not bitter. "Kiss me."

Alex's lips were on his.

Their lips slid together slowly at first, as if trying to relearn each other. It had been years, after all, and a lot of kisses since then with other men.

That distance was forgotten in seconds. Alex's kiss was sweet at first, all lips rubbing and gentle caresses of teeth against Thomas's lower lip. Then, it grew dirtier. Alex's tongue pressed at Thomas's lip, then teased the tip.

Alex tangled his hand in the hair at the back of Thomas's head. Alex pulled him in, their noses bumping. He pulled back enough to shift his weight until he straddled Thomas's lap.

Thomas burned with heat as he grabbed Alex's shoulder blades to yank him closer. He ran one hand down that muscled back. His hand swooped down the curve of Alex's spine into the small of his back. As Alex shivered, Thomas cupped Alex's ass and squeezed.

Alex moaned his approval. Their fronts pressed together with heat. Too many clothes were in the way, but Thomas appreciated the teasing heat of the warm, solid body against his own. He was breathless as Alex kissed him again, his eyes fluttering closed for a minute to enjoy it.

Alex's cock pressed against his own through layers of denim and fabric.

Oh, Christ. I want it. Thomas's breath caught in his throat and he rolled his head back to try to keep his chest from heaving. Alex was having none of it, though; he kept kissing Thomas's neck and throat. He was seeking out those spots...

He does remember!

Alex's lips landed just beneath his ear. Thomas's body jolted and shuddered with pleasure. His cock was achingly hard already, but it twitched particularly at that move. Gentle sucking against that spot made nerves spark to life. His fingertips tingled as Alex moaned and pulled back.

"C-Come upstairs," Thomas whispered. He pushed at the solid weight of Alex's body until Alex decided to shift and stand up. Alex's hand gripped his to pull him up to his feet, and Thomas appreciated it. Being hauled around by him was scorching hot. Like he needed anything else to daydream about.

"I'd be glad to. Show me the way."

Thomas strode up the stairs. He hadn't even made it to the third step before he Alex's hands cupped his ass and swatted it.

"Oi," Thomas laughed, but he was grinning too hard.

"It's just right *there*," Alex protested, following close behind him. "I can't help but admire it."

Thomas shook his head again and tried to speed up his pace. His heart pounded with arousal and thrill and... joy.

This was *fun*. They'd barely even made out, yet already, he was having more fun than with some stranger from a dating site.

Then he stumbled, adrenaline rushing to his head. He grabbed for the handrail and the wall, his foot sliding off the step.

A strong arm had him around the waist and hauled him back to his feet. Alex's other hand was on his chest, helping him straighten up. "Careful there," Alex teased. "I don't want to use my first aid training."

"Of course you have first aid training," Thomas grumbled. He deflected attention from his racing heart and flushed cheeks. His already-hard cock pulsed and throbbed, the sudden shock giving him a little extra blood flow.

"I can give you mouth-to-mouth."

Thomas reached the top of the stairs. Alex still had his fingers hooked through Thomas's belt loops to keep him close. He rolled his eyes at Alex. "I don't want to bust a lung."

"Just a nut."

"Alex!" Thomas's cheeks were hot, but he laughed despite himself. "Christ, you've got the same old attitude."

Alex winked. "I think that was your favorite part of me. Well, second-favorite."

Thomas grabbed Alex and shoved him through the doorway. He kicked the bedroom door shut. "Get in here and shut up."

"Gladly," Alex whispered. He pinned Thomas against the door. Their bodies burned as they both moaned through the silence of the bedroom. The light wasn't even on yet. Alex grabbed Thomas's hands, lacing their fingers together... He pulled both hands above Thomas's head to pin him there and kissed him slow and *filthy*.

"Hnnh," Thomas moaned through the kiss, pushing forward to suck on Alex's lips. He couldn't breathe already, his body burning with need. "Fuck..."

"Wha'?" Alex whispered and kissed. His breath was warm on Thomas's swollen lips. He ground his hard cock against Thomas's, through their jeans.

Thomas shook his head. He didn't even know what to ask for; his mind spun too much. Hazy memories of the Alex before were gone now. It was all *this* Alex, here and hot, his body hard all over and eyes twinkling with mischief. "You're a cocky bastard."

"Mmhmm." Alex yanked him away from the door, steering him over to the bed. It was all Thomas could do to grab Alex's shoulders and pull him along when Alex pushed him down on the bed. They fell together, their legs tangling for a moment, hands already pushing at each other's clothes.

Thomas couldn't stop watching Alex's body, as it was revealed, piece by piece, once again. His chest rippled with new muscles. His stomach, tense with arousal, showed off at least a six-pack. His nipples poked through the cool bedroom air. They just begged to be sucked.

Thomas fought his shirt off and tossed it aside, watching Alex's eyes darken with hunger and scan him from head to toe.

"You always were, but you're still fuckin' hot," Alex whispered. "Just wanna eat you up."

The delicious promise had Thomas's toes curling into the

bed. He wouldn't complain if Alex wanted to suck him off first or kiss him all over... tease him...

"You can do whatever you like," Thomas murmured. "As long as you fuck me, too."

Alex's eyes widened as he caught Thomas's eyes. "Really?" So he remembered their history as well as Thomas.

"I like it," Thomas nodded.

Alex snorted. "I told you, you would. How long did you wait?"

"'Til I went to Halifax... two years after you left." For the first time, the words didn't even have a barb behind them.

Alex raised his eyebrows, then leaned down to kiss Thomas's chest. "Was it worth the wait?"

"Not really."

Alex barked with sudden, surprised laughter. Thomas's brutal honesty had always been a great source of pleasure for him. "Oh. Sorry." He licked around Thomas's nipple, then kissed his chest back up to the hollow at the base of Thomas's throat.

"It's okay. It got better and better. I like it now," Thomas murmured. "I just don't... hook up a lot these days. I had a year or two of it in Halifax, and that was it."

Alex looked thoughtful. Thomas leaned in to grab his cheeks and tilt his head up to kiss those beautiful, pink lips. "What?"

"I've... been cutting back, too," Alex admitted. "I did a lot in Ontario, and..." he trailed off, then just kissed Thomas instead.

Thomas understood. He'd always suspected a part of Alex was compensating for some hidden fears. Like he tried to prove to himself that he deserved the ego he had. There was

a man behind that cocky facade that wanted to settle down...
someday.

Alex was avoiding eye contact, so Thomas took the pressure off. "You gonna take my jeans off or make me rut against you like we're in the backseat of your car again?"

"Demanding," Alex grinned. He grabbed Thomas's belt and pulled it open. Those broad, yet graceful hands worked quickly. He teased the zipper down and stripped the fabric from Thomas's tingling skin. Alex pulled underwear and socks down with jeans to leave him naked.

Thomas didn't feel vulnerable for a second. Instead, he grabbed at Alex's belt, too, and popped it open, then his jeans button, then the buttons of his fly. Alex bucked with his hands to help him get the fabric down to his mid-thighs, then took over to kick everything off.

Alex was hard already, his cock bobbing free in the air. Thomas had almost forgotten how fuckin' big he was. It was impossible to miss when that thick length rubbed against the inside of his hip and his inner thigh. Alex settled down on top of him to kiss him a few more times.

As Alex's body settled on his own and blanketed him, Thomas's skin burned in every spot where they touched. Their chests, their stomachs, their thighs, even their ankles and arms and hands tingled...

Alex's fingers laced between his own again. Alex pinned his hands above his head to kiss him nice and slowly.

This time, with his cock free and pressed between their stomachs, it was less of a tease. Thomas thrust his hips up in a few short, sharp thrusts, grinding against Alex to tease him into action.

"Got condoms and stuff?" Alex murmured.

"All my *stuff* is in a box in the bedside table. Top drawer."

"Clever. Good place for stuff."

Thomas snorted. "Thanks. Choose whatever stuff you want." Alex pulled open the drawer, then fished around until he found the little box. That was where Thomas kept condoms, lube, tissues, and a couple other odds and ends.

"Really? Going Better Homes and Gardens with your condoms? Fancy-ass."

"It's fuckin' navy blue." With floral print, yes, but navy blue nonetheless.

"How adorable."

"Fuck off," Thomas groaned.

Alex set the box on the bedside table and pulled the lid open, then grabbed a condom and lube. He was still laughing as he set everything down next to Thomas and scooted back down to lie against him again.

Thomas ground against him and grabbed the lube. "God, you're insufferable."

"Sorry," Alex grinned. He plucked the bottle out of Thomas's hand. "I wanna do that."

Thomas hadn't expected that. "Really?"

"Yeah. It's half the fun, watching you get more and more desperate..." Alex rubbed his wet fingers together and put the bottle aside. He leaned down to kiss the corner of Thomas's lips. "Besides," he breathed against them. Cool fingers circled his opening to warm up first and Thomas caught his breath. "I wanna make you feel good."

Thomas didn't object. He breathed out slowly as Alex's thick fingers pushed inside. He twitched involuntarily once or twice, then groaned. Alex pushed past the tightness and inside.

God, this already felt incredible, but Thomas couldn't wait to feel *more*. He moved his hips in slow circles, working them with Alex's fingers to let Alex thrust inside in a slow, steady rhythm. Each firm brush of fingers across the sensitive spot inside made his body jolt just a little harder.

By the time Alex pulled his fingers out, Thomas squirmed against the bed with need. His cock throbbed and his head spun. His eyes were closed tightly with pleasure as he dug his fingers into the bed and tried to catch his breath. A packet crinkled, and then there was a muffled gasp and the slick sound of a man stroking himself with a little more lube.

Only the feeling of a warm, thick tip pressing between his legs broke his momentary reverie. Thomas snapped his eyes open to get a good look at Alex's cock as it pushed into him.

"Hnnh," Thomas groaned quietly, running a hand down his own stomach until he circled his fingers around Alex's shaft. He teasingly stroked down to the latex-covered base and squeezed lightly. Alex still pushed inside, and he finally had to pull his hand away and grab Alex's ass instead.

"You're a little tease," Alex breathed into his ear. His own breathing came in quick, harsh pants already. "I forgot."

"I have my – nnh – moments," Thomas moaned. "Come on. Fuck me."

Alex laughed breathlessly and braced himself on his knees. He laced their hands together once more and thrust in short, sharp movements.

Each time Alex's thick cock sank a little further into him, Thomas groaned his approval. He wasn't quiet in bed; at least, not when he was being pleased this thoroughly.

When Alex's lips met his again, Thomas was glad to kiss back. He lost himself in the moment, pushing up into Alex with each thrust as his head spun with pleasure. His whole body was already tight and hot, but he didn't want to come right away.

He'd waited fucking long enough for this. He had to make it last.

Alex's thrusts into him were quick and deep. Each time he buried himself inside Thomas, Thomas was satiated for a brief moment. How hot and filling and *thick* Alex felt...

The bed creaked under them. Seconds or minutes passed with shared quick breaths and kisses. They brushed their lips along each other's neck, shoulders, face, and most of all, lips. And Alex's touches... Only one of Alex's hands curled tightly against his, their fingers laced together so hard his hands tingled.

The other wandered across Thomas's body, tweaking his nipple and rubbing along his ribs. Alex explored every inch of skin. "I'm gonna come soon," Thomas laughed breathlessly. "Especially if you keep--"

That palm cupped his erection and squeezed hard.

"Hnnh!"

"Oh?" Alex grinned. "If you're gonna come, I'd better get to work..." He was breathless and his cheeks were flushed, his eyes a little too hazy. He was so on edge too.

Thomas wrested one hand free to dig his nails into Alex's back. He groaned loudly when a tight ring of fingers slid down his cock and back up. Alex twisted his hand with each upstroke... His body was tensing, shuddering involuntarily. "Jesus, Alex, I... yes...!"

"Come for me, baby," Alex breathed out. His thumb ran across the head and around before he pumped his hand up and down again.

While Alex's dick drove into him, his firm and gentle guiding hand pulled Thomas along. His body was already burning with heat at Alex's closeness and the intimacy between them...

Thomas came hard, losing all awareness of anything but the insistent throbbing, spurting pleasure. It started deep in his belly and shuddered through his whole body. Alex kept stroking him with each squirt to coax out the last of his pleasure, and Thomas blushed hard.

His fingers and toes tingled, his muscles clenching and releasing as his mind spun. He couldn't remember the last time it had been this good. When he finally collapsed on the bed again, Thomas pulled his other hand away from Alex's. He cupped the back of his head to kiss him hard, in silent thanks.

"Gorgeous," Alex breathed out, and only now was Thomas aware of how rough and tight his voice was. He must have been barely holding back himself.

Thomas slapped Alex's ass and moaned. "Yes... You're almost there. C'mon, Alex..."

"Thom--" Alex bit back his cry but a strangled groan slipped out regardless. His skin beaded with sweat, cheeks red with exertion. His eyes were hazy, yet fixed entirely on Thomas. Like Thomas was the most beautiful, sexy sight Alex dreamt up to push him over the edge of climax.

Thomas smiled as Alex's hips shuddered and stuttered. Alex buried his face in Thomas's neck with each irregular, deep thrust of his hips. He wrapped his arms around Alex to pull him close, rubbing his hand up and down his back and kissing at his neck. "That's it," Thomas whispered. "Mm, fuck, you feel incredible..."

"S-So do you. Christ," Alex whispered as he gave one or two last little jerky thrusts, then tried desperately to catch his breath. He pushed himself up on an elbow and gazed off, then shook his head as he looked down at Thomas again.

Thomas grinned, letting him pull back and clean up the

condom. He just stretched out on the bed, pulling Alex closer again to cuddle into his side.

Alex wrapped one strong arm around Thomas's side to rub his back while he pecked his lips. He was the one to break the silence a few moments later. "Glad you texted me."

"Yeah," Thomas whispered. His body was warm and satisfied, the urge to sleep tickling at the edges of his mind. He ignored that for now. "Things were pretty hectic. They're quieter now."

It was bizarre how comfortable he felt telling Alex all his worries, filling him in on family news. If he was gonna be pissed at Alex, he should've been properly distant. But no — he wanted to be close, and it just felt right to talk to him.

"Mmhmm?" Alex murmured. "Your brother doing better? Family all right?"

"Yeah, and yeah. Surgery went great for Cam. Jackson's business is good. Noah's doing a couple shows a season, and Chase has a great portfolio going. Everyone's doing good..."

"And you?"

Thomas gazed into Alex's eyes, resisting the urge to ask why Alex cared that much. It was enough that he did. "Not bad. Going for a promotion at work, when I can."

"To what?"

"Whatever I can get," Thomas smiled. "I didn't get a degree for nothing."

"You went to college in Halifax?"

"Mmhmm. Two years in finance."

Alex smiled, and it was easy to tell he was feeling a bit proud. "You'll get a promotion sooner or later then. You're more than qualified."

"Other than that, not a lot going on with me since we last talked," Thomas admitted. "Things have been... quiet."

"Romantically?"

Thomas furrowed his brow. That made it sound like Alex was interested, but that goddamn face of his was so hard to read. Probably harder, now that he was an investigator and a professional liar. "Yeah, there's nobody right now. If you weren't such a dick, I'd consider dating you."

Alex's face cracked in a smile, and then he snorted with laughter and rolled onto his back. Thomas glowered at how easily he took the accusation, like he didn't care... or like it was true. "For the record, there's not much going on with me either. Just... work and seeing family now and then."

"Sounds boring," Thomas commented.

"Work's exciting enough. I don't mind boring now and then," Alex smiled. He sat up and Thomas eased himself up on his elbow, then pushed himself upright, too. "Speaking of which, I should get going. One or two more things to clear up."

This was it, then. The moment they had to figure out what the fuck they'd do next. Thomas pulled on his jeans, zipping them up with extra care. He watched Alex get dressed in a flash, his hands almost flying up the buttons. It wasn't like he was rushing it; he was just good at this. How many other one-night stands had he had in Ontario? Probably more men than Thomas had taken home in Halifax.

They were quiet while he led Alex downstairs. When they got to the door, Thomas paused to lean in the foyer while Alex put his coat and shoes on.

Thomas's heart drummed when Alex straightened up again slowly. It was hard to tell if it was anxiety, excitement, or both making his heart flutter again. Thomas's eyes fell to Alex's lips.

Alex leaned in slowly, cupping Thomas's cheek and

giving him a moment to pull back. When he didn't, Alex kissed him tenderly.

Despite his best efforts, Thomas slumped a little against the wall, letting Alex step closer and kiss him again, pinning him there. They kissed a third time as their thighs nestled and Alex's thumb rubbed his cheek. He could honest-to-God lose himself in this man, the way he kissed him... all gentle lips, warm breaths, teases of teeth and tongue...

Then Alex pulled back. Thomas hastily straightened up again, blinking away the momentary haze. "See you around," Alex murmured.

Thomas cleared his throat. "See you." He stepped back while Alex pulled open the door.

Their eyes met for a moment and Alex nodded. Then he was gone, the door closed, and Thomas leaned his head on the wall with a quiet thump.

He hadn't dated a lot of men – just a handful of serious relationships, none of which had lasted more than a few months. Even so, Thomas knew damn well that kiss hadn't been a "goodbye, have a good life" kiss on either of their parts.

What was he supposed to do with this?

CHAPTER
Eight

ALEX

OF COURSE DARREN'S CAR WASN'T IN THE APARTMENT PARKING lot.

Alex thumped his forehead against the wheel. He'd just done a third circuit of the lot to check for the cheating bastard's red Volvo. Well, he co-owned it with his wife, but he'd probably get it in the divorce when it went to court.

There was a fresh dump of a few inches of snow, but it couldn't possibly be one of the cars buried under the whole night's accumulation. Darren couldn't have gotten home before ten. He wasn't in his usual spot, and he hadn't chosen any other spot either. So where was he?

Just as Alex was worrying, he spotted movement from the parking lot entrance and went still. The red car pulled into the lot and into Darren's usual spot while Alex sat in the guest parking space. Alex raised his camera, his heart jolting with anticipation that *something* was going on.

He wasn't wrong. Rather than a late-night grocery run or pizza craving, Darren apparently hadn't been satisfied with Anna. A young redhead was on his arm, dressed like she'd been out at a club – stilettos, short dress, neon paper wrist-band. To Alex, that band identified which club she'd been at.

"Oh, honey," Alex whispered, shaking his head as he zoomed in. This one definitely didn't know he was married with the way her arm was wrapped around his. Alex rolled down the window just enough to slip the mic out, then caught a giggle and a snippet of voices.

"I live on the sixth floor... apartment nine..."

Liar. He was on the third floor in apartment one, right over the guest parking spot. From this spot, there was a perfect view up into the bedroom window. The same bedroom Darren shared with his wife when she wasn't away.

"No, I'm just joking. I wanted to see if you'd blush."

They disappeared inside the building.

Christ, what an idiot. It wasn't just a slip-up or an affair with someone better suited to him – a mistake, but *almost* understandable. That was, if Anna was some horrible controlling woman, which she didn't seem to be.

No, to Darren, this was sex for the sake of getting his dick wet. Alex almost bared his teeth. He set down the micro-phone, stopped recording, and refocused on the bedroom window. He hated these guys, and he hated having to show their wives the evidence later.

Not that Alex had always been a shining star of morality, but Christ, he'd never knowingly cheated. As a honey trap, it had always been a job done *for* the partner, with limits set by his client. Darren was just playing these women, including his own wife. *That* was an asshole move, and he deserved to lose the Volvo.

Darren didn't even close the damn blinds before pushing his fling's dress up. The bedroom lamp was on, so the silhou-ettes against the sheer curtains showed everything. Alex recorded visual, though the windows were closed against the January cold. He wasn't going to get any audio. Not that he needed it with video this good.

When they went out of sight, presumably for the bed, he still waited in case there was any more evidence. Now, he had time for his mind to wander.

Thomas had been so good. Way better than he remembered – not that he'd ever let Alex get *that* far before. And suddenly he wanted it now? Alex wasn't complaining. Better late than never. And maybe he'd call him again...

Alex realized that something in his heart was... he didn't want to say *fluttering*, but it was.

He didn't believe in love, really, or even long-term happiness. He'd seen too many couples dissolve. Yet as he waited for more evidence of this woman he hadn't connected with Darren before, he wondered. Maybe he just saw the worst side of things – people sneaking around behind their spouses' backs. Even when he found no evidence of cheating, there was some underlying trust issue. Something always made the client call him in the first place.

He never got hired to spy on *great* marriages or relationships between couples who finished one another's sentences.

Alex was smiling.

"Christ," he muttered, rubbing his face. "It was just a... hookup."

With his ex. The one he'd always had in the back of his mind, whenever he'd dated a man for more than two or three months... The one who'd rejected him when he came back to town. Who had made it clear he could fuck off. Until tonight, when he'd flat-out wanted Alex to fuck him.

And it wasn't just sex. Anyone could see that from a mile

off. The chemistry before they'd even touched, the way they'd held each other afterward...

Alex wanted more than Thomas could give him.

Not even an hour later, Alex recorded the other woman getting in a taxi and leaving. He called it quits and headed to bed. He had to talk to Lexy, Darren's poor wife, tomorrow and show her this bullshit.

One thought wouldn't leave his head the whole time. As he walked through the stinging cold to his front door, he wondered: was Thomas the one that got away?

CHAPTER
Nine

THOMAS

CHRIST.

He couldn't tell his brothers yet.

This was either the best or the stupidest thing he'd done in his life, and Thomas still wasn't sure which.

There was one thing for certain: his idea about getting over Alex by sleeping with him hadn't worked. Instead, Alex was on Thomas's mind even more as he went through the workweek with an eye on Thursday, not Friday.

He was in the bar that Wednesday evening with his brothers and friends. Well, mostly his brothers' friends, though they had become his own over the last year. As he thought, Thomas tuned them out for the most part. He was too busy thinking about the possibilities for tomorrow.

Maybe they'd see each other and there'd be another spark of chemistry.

But...

His stomach twisted to think of it, but maybe that was all Alex had ever wanted.

"Huh? Yeah," Thomas agreed when he heard his name, looking around at the others.

Floyd was chuckling at him. "You're completely out of it, man. You all right?"

Behind the teasing eyes, there was concern from Chase's boss. Floyd owned Chase's tattoo shop, and he'd come around to hang out with the rest of them these days. "Oh, yeah, I'm fine," he assured him.

"You sure?"

Thomas hesitated for a moment, then shook his head with a smile. If he was going to break down and talk to someone, it should be his brothers. Floyd was the friend he most loosely knew. "Yeah, I'm fine," he said. "But thanks."

Floyd nodded, then glanced back at the table. "They went off on a tangent. Ashley thinks hockey came from Scotland. They're Googling it."

"Oh, Jesus, he challenged Cam?" Thomas laughed. "And Kevin? Good luck."

Ashley, Ryan, Kevin, and Cam were all hunched around Jackson's phone. Noah and Chase rolled their eyes at each other.

"Fuckin' eh?" Kevin exclaimed when the page loaded, and Thomas laughed quietly. He wasn't particularly close to these guys, but at least he had friends to see every week. He was luckier than most. He tried to pay attention as the argument was won with the power of technology.

CHAPTER
Ten

ALEX

"How did you guys know you were right for each other?"

It was a weird question to ask his parents, but Alex was curious. He'd been thinking more about his ideas around romance and marriage, and the inevitable failures of both. His parents *had* been married for almost three decades now.

"Oh, that's easy," his father laughed as he leaned back in his chair. "I met your mother and I wanted to pull my hair out right away."

She rolled her eyes and pretended to throw her newspaper in his direction while Alex laughed. "And I thought he needed swatting like a dog trying to get into the pantry."

They were being lighthearted, and Alex's heart almost hurt. This kind of love was something totally different from what he saw every day on the job.

It was the kind of tender laughter forged by intimacy that he thought he might have shared for a minute with Thomas...

But that was moving way too fast. He swallowed and refocused on them.

He needed a more serious answer. His dad cleared his throat and straightened up when his mom gave him a stern look.

"I think it's what they always say – we just knew. But there was a lot of work that went in behind the scenes to making it work. Compromises, learning to live with differences. And if those differences had been *too* great..."

"We never would have made it this long," Mom agreed.

That was a lot more helpful. "What do you mean? Life values?"

"Yes, and plans. We both wanted a kid, and to raise him a certain way. We wanted to live in the same kind of place and share the same kind of values."

"Things are different for you, though," Dad spoke up. "I assume you're still dating other men..."

Alex laughed, and so did his parents. "Yeah, that hasn't changed."

"Guys can be a little different, you know. We need a little more time to grow up. You're not even halfway through your twenties. Don't feel pressured to settle down. It was normal while we were young, but you can get away with being single a lot longer, until you find the *right* one."

Alex nodded. "It... wasn't just about me," he laughed, lying through his teeth. "Just this weird case."

"Another cheating one?"

"Yeah." Lexy hadn't let him finish the investigation yet. She wanted more, and it was dragging at his newly-improved mood. There were daily ups and downs with his... whatever his depression was, anyway.

"You need to keep taking those cases?"

Alex winced. He couldn't exactly tell his parents why he had to take every case he was offered: because he'd be broke if he didn't. He didn't have a fallback plan. Nobody in Ontario would hire him for an agency, so he'd had to move out here and start his own. It had come out that he was working in a high-end gay boutique in the day and as a gay men's honey trap at night. The jobs were surprisingly compatible.

That had paid wonderfully, but one day he'd just woken up and realized he didn't like it anymore. Plus, he was struggling even to get private event security jobs for straight people, no longer trusted in his own community. Then, he'd given up and moved back here.

He'd told his parents it was all to move back to Fredericton and be closer to them, of course.

Besides... if it weren't for work, he wouldn't have a reason to get out of bed some days.

"Yeah, my business is still pretty new," he nodded. "I can't afford to be picky until at least the first year's up. I'd rather take this kind anyway. You know, I can validate their suspicions when people never had proof..."

His mother nodded. "It seems like it's hard, though."

"It is. This guy... they're only newlyweds, but he's having an affair with one woman *and* bringing home others."

His mother scoffed. "Now *he* needs smacking with a newspaper. Or something harder."

"Mom!" Alex laughed.

"I know *you* can't, dear. I'm just saying."

His father chuckled. "She's right. Not all of us are like that. If you're worried about finding your own--"

"Nah," Alex groaned, but he was paying close attention.

"--all I'm saying is, keep holding on. There might be fewer of you out there, but you'll find one."

"And he'll be the right one, more importantly."

Alex smiled, rising to his feet. "Okay, okay," he laughed. "I gotta get going soon. Thanks, Mom, Dad."

"Anytime. Come over for supper again soon," Dad told him. "Don't burn out."

"I won't."

After his usual goodbyes, Alex sat in the car for a few minutes to warm it up. He leaned against the window.

They were right: there *were* some different men. Thomas, for one. Thomas had been loyal almost to a fault; it would have been much easier to dump him all those years ago if he hadn't been. But being dumped had to hurt even more, so he didn't try to summon up too much sympathy for himself.

He'd been right to look for a relationship that had what he needed, but not in the way he went about it. If he ever dumped someone again, it would be face-to-face, not over the phone. That memory made him cringe.

"Yeah, I *was* that dick, kind of," Alex muttered. Maybe they were right and it did take men a little longer to grow up and be ready to settle down. Maybe he was just getting to that stage now.

Thomas was two years younger. Was he almost ready?

If not... could Alex wait?

His heart raced. He'd never considered that question when it came to any other guy. The fact that he was even thinking about that told him that something was different.

But he couldn't dwell on it. Thomas didn't want more with him.

Alex tried not to think the word *yet* at the end of that sentence. He pulled away from the curb to drive home to his apartment.

<h1>CHAPTER
Eleven</h1>

THOMAS

IF THOMAS SPENT EXTRA TIME IRONING HIS SHIRT FOR Thursday, he wouldn't admit it. When Thursday came around, he brushed his teeth on his lunch break. The time seemed to drag by as the hour approached two o'clock.

Alex was due any time.

Naturally, Thomas was in the middle of serving a client when the handsome man stepped into the bank. A cool breeze blew through the lobby when the door opened, ruffling the waiting area brochures.

The client was slowly entering their PIN, and Thomas had just a second to look up and make eye contact with Alex.

Alex was looking for him, too, his gaze scanning the row of desks before his eyes lit upon Thomas's face.

They shared a look for a moment, their eyes meeting as a slow smile crept across Alex's face. That same slow, charming smile, but there was more sincerity today. Thomas just hoped none of the other tellers were looking between them. The chemistry between them felt like a lethal charge in the air.

Oh, Christ. Thomas's heart downright fluttered, but he ignored it. He wasn't forgiving Alex yet, however sweet he'd been in bed. He drew his lips down and nodded briskly, then returned his attention to the client. Perhaps he paid her a little too much attention, ignoring where Alex went.

Alex would never commit to one guy, would he? And Thomas's family wouldn't approve. Not just because it was Alex, but Jackson always said exes should stay exes.

This thing between them... it was just a slip-up, a mistake Thomas thought would be logical. It had only complicated things.

Thomas's phone vibrated quietly and he ignored it until the last customer was out of sight. Only then were they allowed to check their phones. Well, they were discouraged, but there were slow days where hardly any customers came in. The tellers here had insisted that it was this or Facebook games.

It was a text from Alex.

You look beautiful today.

A blush crept up his cheeks as he scanned the room, trying to look casual. Alex was sitting in the waiting area for bank officer appointments, side-on to him. He had one arm stretched along the back of the comfy leather couch, his gaze fixed on the offices just beyond.

He tapped out a quick response.

Fuck off, you. You know that was one time.

Still, heat crawled up his cheeks and through his stomach. He burned with the desire for Alex to give him another sly look. It made him shudder.

He had to put up walls *now*, or Alex was going to break his heart again.

A minute later, Alex checked his phone. Thomas saw even

from this distance and angle that Alex was smiling. Alex didn't look around at him, which was actually more maddening.

Thomas had no idea why his heart was racing so much. He wasn't the type to flirt by playing hard-to-get. What had gotten into him, apart from the obvious joke?

As Thomas tidied up his desk, keeping Alex in his peripheral vision, Alex stood up and stretched. The self-assured man wandered around to pick up brochures from each table and scan them. He looked left and right, probably for a bathroom, before taking a quick wander down an aisle.

Wrong way, Thomas thought. He wanted to gloat at Alex getting turned around when he was proud of being so good with directions and building layouts. But no, he wasn't going to interact.

It took Thomas a minute to realize Alex hadn't come back.

Fuck. He's investigating. Not in my workplace. Thomas's blood ran hot with annoyance. He hadn't come to make an appointment, or... see him. No, that was a stupid thought, but the synchronicity of bumping into Alex *had* been a little hard to believe.

He stood up, moving the bar across his counter and glancing at his coworkers. Chris and Georgie were both there to handle any unexpected rushes. "Be right back."

"Yep," Chris said without taking his eyes off his phone screen while Georgie nodded.

Thomas strode across the marble floor of the lobby. His shoes clicked against the tiles as he made his way directly to the offices. Maggie wasn't at the desk; she was probably fighting the copy machine again today.

Alex was lurking near the offices, turning this way and

that. He looked lost despite how small the maze of cubicles and offices really was.

"Hello," Thomas greeted, his voice clipped. He approached Alex like any other client – albeit with a bit more sternness.

Alex had a moment of looking guilty before smiling. "Sorry, I got a bit lost." He turned slowly away from Anna's office and raised a hand.

Then, Thomas's breath caught in his throat.

Anna's office blinds were closed, but one of the blinds around chest level was ajar. Through that, he caught a glimpse of something he really *hadn't* wanted to see. Anna was facing away, but a guy sat on her desk, his shirt unbuttoned and fingers digging into the desk. Including his ring finger, with a ring on it.

"What the--" he cut himself off, his gaze flickering away as he blushed hard. "Is she seeing some..." he trailed off. Alex was an investigator. He'd needed an appointment at this time. He was lingering outside this office.

Ohhh, no.

Even if the ethics code didn't prohibit this, basic workplace decency did.

Alex didn't answer. He shrugged. "I'd better sit down and wait for... Lisa, I think it was."

"Yes." Thomas stiffly led Alex back to the waiting area without answering. Alex fidgeted with his phone in his breast pocket.

Just before they emerged, Alex touched Thomas's arm slightly to stop him. He kept his voice to a murmur. "See? My work *can* be good."

Thomas couldn't disagree; lending to a client you were cheating with was a major breach of the ethics code. There was no way management knew about this. Anna wouldn't be employed if they'd known.

Was he supposed to tell? If he didn't... If anyone ever investigated, he couldn't say he hadn't known. For god's sake, Alex could be investigating that very moment. And more than that, it was about doing the right thing. He just wasn't sure whether that was what he thought it was.

Alex sank into the couch again. "Thank you for your assistance." Maggie was coming back with Lisa, who smiled in greeting to Alex. He rose to his feet again. "Ah, hello."

Unseen, Thomas walked quietly back to his workstation.

He wasn't a snitch, but he also wasn't dishonest... and there might be major fraud happening. Or just one little house loan. No, one loan wasn't better than ten or twenty. His head spun.

This wasn't how he'd expected Thursday to go, but he was still glad he'd dressed up neatly. Alex's suit had been freshly-pressed today. In thinking that, Thomas dared to think he wouldn't have been out of place on Alex's arm.

Not the time.

But if he reported and the wrong person heard, if Anna *was* being protected by people higher up... Thomas might be out of a job, and without a reference for another.

And he couldn't afford that.

He had some big decisions to make.

CHAPTER
Twelve

ALEX

ANY DAY ALEX GOT HOME EARLY WAS A GREAT DAY. HE HAD the evidence Lexy wanted that there *was* an affair with one woman. He'd still have to go out on Saturday to catch them romancing each other on the trails, though. Lexy was obsessed with proving that this wasn't a one-time mistake.

From what she'd said, the asshole had always excused himself by saying it wasn't anything serious, just self-control slips. Alex hoped catching Darren a couple times with the same woman would blow a hole in Lexy's ability to forgive him for those "mistakes" he kept making.

He settled down by grabbing a beer from the fridge and chilling out in front of the TV. There was a marathon of some show about hot lawyers, so he watched that.

A little later, Alex ate a microwave supper he'd grabbed on his way home, and then returned to the marathon. He had a slight interest in the exploits of the characters, at least one of whom was *clearly* fucking gay. The TV would never show that, though.

Alex chilled out, doing as little as possible until he got a text from Thomas that evening.

Call me?

He grinned and licked his teeth, stretching out again to enjoy the moment. The same man who'd told him to fuck off that afternoon was all hot and cold. Clearly he was getting to Thomas somehow. It was kind of enjoyable since Thomas had always been able to keep him at arms-length.

"Hello, Thomas," Alex greeted once his ex answered. He knew he sounded a little smug, but he couldn't help it.

Thomas sounded annoyed. "Look, this isn't another..."

"Booty call?"

"Shut up. I'm only calling because I want to know about your work."

Alex straightened up. That was less fun. He rubbed his hand back through his hair and muted the TV. "Go on."

"Are you bringing what we saw to the bank's attention?"

Alex paused, considering how to answer this. Thomas knew who he'd been investigating, but not why. He could have been working for the bank, a partner if Anna one, or Darren's wife as he actually was. Thomas wouldn't be able to guess which, and he had to keep it that way.

"I can't. This is evidence in an ongoing investigation."

Thomas paused for a few long moments. "Ah." He sounded frustrated. "Right."

"Anyone who sees impropriety in the workplace can approach their supervisor," Alex said mildly, tugging his jeans and scratching his thigh. "Naturally."

"Ah... Right." Thomas paused for a few long moments and Alex let him stew in silence before he spoke up again. "I do approve of catching fraudsters and cheaters and stuff, I guess. It's just that we were on the receiving end of it before."

Alex hadn't expected any forgiveness, even unspoken. "Oh? I'm glad you see a different side now."

"But you *really* shouldn't have crept on Cam if you still wanted anything to do with me," Thomas told him. "You had to know he wouldn't like that."

"Yeah, I... had some warning he might not take it well." Alex had been told that by the guys who'd hired him. He'd had an idea anyway, from his own general knowledge of Thomas's brothers. "I was wrong to put anyone you love on surveillance. I hesitated before taking the job, but... I should have turned it down. I know you might not trust me again and that's okay. I just... needed the money, man."

"Damn right that's okay," Thomas told him firmly. "I get needing the money... a little more now." Alex frowned, concerned for a brief moment before Thomas went on. "But I already didn't trust you."

Alex's annoyance slipped through for the first time in a long time. He was used to being utterly professional and keeping his feelings under wraps. But Thomas *kept* poking that damn wound. "Still banging on about me leaving for Toronto?"

"Excuse me?"

"You were the one who didn't want to be out," Alex pointed out mildly. He knew it would piss Thomas off, but he couldn't help saying it. "I warned you I needed to be public if I was gonna date you exclusively. And you knew I was graduating and leaving."

"So it's my fault now?"

Alex pictured that indignant face. "It would have happened one way or another if you never got the balls to come out. I saved us the agony later." The phone line went dead; he knew it before he even tested. "Thomas? You there?"

He laughed quietly and tossed his phone on the couch. It was damn hard to get Thomas worked up at all, let alone to the point where he'd hang up on him.

As much as he tried to ignore it, remorse crept in moments later, though. Provoking Thomas also wasn't much fun. He liked the adrenaline rush of getting one over on someone, sure. But this was the guy he wanted to rekindle something with...

It was a stupid call, and Alex regretted it within ten seconds. He turned the TV up again, letting Thomas take the space he needed. When he was ready to talk, he'd call back – maybe next week, maybe never.

It was harsh, but it was the truth; he'd needed someone he could be out with, and Thomas hadn't been that guy. Nonetheless, he knew he could have put it a little better. Okay, a lot better.

That was a truth Alex was reluctant to admit: he was a hard man to be around. The lower his mood, the more he poked and prodded people, and damn it, he didn't even know why.

Probably another depression symptom. He made a face. *I'll make an appointment someday.*

And Thomas was right – he had to look harder at the cases he took from now on, and maybe at how much of a dick people saw him as. He was never gonna get a boyfriend if he kept this act up. A bad boy was only good for one thing, and Thomas had already gotten that.

Maybe I'll make an appointment tomorrow.

Alex rolled over to grab his phone and dial the doctor's office. It was way past closing, but they'd get the message and call him back.

"Hello. I'm looking to make an appointment. My number

is..." Alex tried to sound perky as he left the message, then pressed *hang up* and put the phone down again.

If Alex ever wanted more... he had to give more, too.

CHAPTER
Thirteen

CAM

Mom and Dad were in the kitchen, and Jackson was helping them wash up. Cameron had Thomas alone in the living room. He intended to take advantage of the moment's peace and quiet. After all, a little birdie had told him that Thomas might *not* be opposed to dating right now.

He and Noah had discussed the possibility of setting Thomas up with someone – one of their mutual friends or someone new.

But first, it only seemed right to chat to him about it.

"So, Valentine's Day is only next month," Cam tried, stretching his legs out as he sprawled on the couch.

Thomas gave him a disbelieving look. "That's about the least subtle way you could have put it."

Cameron laughed and rubbed his face. "Yeah. So, you planning on getting a move on before then? Or are you waiting for the perfect person to slide down the sidewalk into your lap?" It was possible Thomas was suffering from unrealistic standards, after all. It was pretty hard to beat

Noah and Chase as being the perfect boyfriends. Noah a little more perfect, though.

"Mm," Thomas glanced out into the backyard, then looked back at Cam. "What I told you about after the barbecue in August, that kind of panned out, but kind of didn't."

Vague. Still, at least Thomas was talking, and Cam wanted to encourage it. Maybe he was shy about talking about a girlfriend when everything else in the family was about boyfriends. Cam didn't want him hiding away his personal life. Or, of course, it could be a boyfriend...

"You ever call them back, then?"

Thomas was quiet.

"You gotta take initiative sometimes," Cameron elbowed Thomas. "Dude, it's been months."

"That's what Noah said."

"Aha, you've been talking to love guru Noah but not your own brother?" Cam feigned being wounded. "Or even Jackson, the lump..."

Thomas was frowning. "Yeah."

"Why not?"

"You can drop this subject anytime."

Cam raised his eyebrow. "Why?"

Thomas turned to look him dead in the eye. "Just mind your own business. I asked you back then not to interfere. So don't interfere."

That was about as close as Thomas ever got to yelling at someone. Cameron instantly put up his hand and nodded. "Yeah. Sure. Sorry, man."

Thomas's shoulders sank and he rolled them a little, then offered a smile instead. "Yeah."

The silence between them was tense, interrupted only by clattering and laughter from the kitchen.

Cam snorted and poked his finger in Thomas's direction, waving it around his chest. "You've got a little pent-up..."

Thomas slapped his hand away and punched his shoulder. "Says the one who was grouchy for *months* last year."

"Well, they fixed *that*, at least," Cam smirked just to make Thomas groan. Being able to have great, rowdy, red-blooded sex with Noah again was a treat. Cam had noticed that he was a lot calmer in general, so Thomas wasn't wrong. Maybe Thomas needed to get laid, too. "You know, you can take up a sport," Cam suggested.

"What?" Thomas had never really *done* sports. "Like what? Hockey?"

"Fuck, no. They'd crush you," Cam laughed. "You're living in the capital of outdoor sports. Snowshoeing or skiing or something. We have enough of the shit around to do something with. Arctic ice running."

"Is that a sport?"

"It should be. That'd be hilarious. Even more injuries than hockey, I bet."

Thomas rolled his eyes but still smiled. "Fine. I've been thinking about going out this weekend and doing something just to..." he trailed off for a moment, then finished, "do something."

Get your mind off something? Ooh, Cam was intrigued. He knew better than to push Thomas's buttons again so soon. "Yeah, you should. Some quiet time alone might be good. Or around other people. You spend enough damn time alone."

"I have friends. At the bank, and the board game cafe when I go."

"Like once a month, when you're not reading the latest... I don't know, horror-thriller thing."

Thomas shoved him. "I hate horror. You should know that."

"Whatever the hell you read," Cam grinned. "Nerd."

Thomas hauled himself to his feet and shook his head. "We should see if they need any help. God, you're like the cat who got the canary since surgery. I think you need a little less activity."

Cam laughed richly. "No way. I waited fuckin' long enough," he shook his head. "Hey, maybe sports will help you meet someone and get a little *more* activity. Meet me in the middle," he wriggled his eyebrows.

"I'm ignoring you until further notice," Thomas shook his head. Cam laughed again and followed his little brother to the kitchen. They'd all find out what Thomas was hiding eventually. Maybe before his deathbed, Cam thought with a grin. He had to open up *someday*, to someone. Hopefully they'd be included.

CHAPTER
Fourteen

ALEX

"So, I need to go up around that way? Is there anything that way?"

Alex knew damn well that there were warm-up cabins in both directions from the trailhead. He just needed to confirm which trail the romantic couple had chosen for their planned illicit rendezvous.

He was pretty sure he knew which direction they'd gone, but he had to be sure. Skiing in the wrong direction would be a pretty big fuck-up.

"Well," the ski rental guy said, rubbing his chin, "there's a cabin both ways, if you get that far out. But for your first time on skis in a while, you might not." Alex might have feigned a little less knowledge than he had to flirt more with the guy. Nothing wrong with that, even if it was idle interest.

It was weird only to have a passing interest in the guy before losing interest again. His days of eying men who walked into the high-end boutique where he'd started his career, and of getting at least three numbers a shift, were over.

"Oh," Alex laughed. "I guess you must have regulars who can. Do they come out on weekends, or is it amateurs like me?"

"There's one couple who seem talented. They came this morning and headed up to the Sycamore cabin. You might want to go to the Beech cabin..." the guy hinted with a rueful laugh.

"Is-- wait, isn't that against the rules or something?"

"They look like a new couple, I don't recognize them. The regulars know better," the rental guy grinned. "When a marathon skier crashes in with snot running down his face and interrupts--"

"Oh, *Jesus*," Alex laughed, holding up a hand. "That was an image I didn't want." He almost doubled over on his poles, trying desperately to forget it. "Fuck." The guy was leaning on the table as he laughed, too. "They've never been out before and they made it there? I might have a shot."

"This is... maybe the third time I've seen them, but yeah, they found it easy enough. They said last time they enjoyed it..." the guy ruefully smiled. "That trail *is* flatter and a bit faster."

"Okay. I might give it a shot. I'll just knock before I enter." Alex winked, pushing himself gently backward on his skis. "Thanks a lot."

The guy was cute enough, bearded and young with dark brown eyes, but so not Alex's type. Nothing like Thomas, either.

"You're welcome. Enjoy your afternoon."

Alex turned like a starfish, one step at a time, until he faced the trailhead. He glided away across the snow in small, testing strides.

It was easier than he remembered, but he'd strain some

muscles he wasn't used to targeting in the gym. He had to pace himself to make it all the way to the cabin. Alex desperately wanted to gather that last bit of evidence for Lexy and wrap up his case.

It only took a few glides from foot to foot as he settled into the easy, smooth rocking rhythm. The rental guy had waxed them with exactly the right stuff. He had just enough grip when he needed it, but enough glide to skate across the top of the snow. He'd make better time than he could in the classic tracks with his skis parallel and his arms working too hard.

With leg muscles like his, he kept his strides under control. It was a joy to skate across the crisp, squeaking, white groomed trail until the main cabin vanished behind him.

The most exertion wasn't even in his legs. It was in his arms each time he dug his pole tips into the snow and bent. He propelled himself along as his skis formed a V enveloping the direction he wanted to travel. He rocked back onto his right foot without poling each time, then dug his poles in again for his left foot.

For extra speed, he *could* double-pole and propel himself along on both left and right strides. He didn't have to go that fast right now, though. He'd watched them set off just a few minutes ago and they couldn't be a lot faster than him.

The trees closed in around him within minutes and he was utterly alone. Well, almost alone. Birdsong reached his ears, from winter birds braving warmer weather to forage. Probably partridges or jays. The tree boughs hung heavy with snow, a few bright berries peeking out between the lumps of snow and icicles. The last freezing rain had at least given a great, crisp surface to the snow that made skiing easier. It dragged trees down sometimes in the dead of winter, so it wasn't always great.

Oddly enough, this was the most peaceful he remembered being since moving here from the hustle of Toronto's suburbs. The air bit at his nose and lungs, but he wrapped his scarf a little tighter. He clutched his ski poles tightly to keep propelling himself forward.

The solitude was kind of nice, even if part of him wanted to share it with someone – to point out pretty Christmas card scenes or split snacks with. And if that someone was Thomas in his idle daydreams, nobody had to know.

Thomas still hadn't called him, but it had only been two days since their Thursday evening call. He expected it would take another day or two for Thomas to cool off again. When he did, Alex would apologize. He *had* been in the wrong, at least partly, for that conversation.

But that would happen in time. Right now, he was just a few easy miles away from nailing this bastard exactly how Lexy wanted, getting a great paycheck, and helping her get the confidence to confront him with the damning evidence he was so sloppily giving to him on a platter.

It was hard to say which gave him more pleasure: the beauty and solitude of the woods or getting to ski on the clock. Maybe both.

He loved his life sometimes.

Fifteen

THOMAS

HE COULDN'T POSSIBLY NEED ANYTHING ELSE. HE HAD SKI pants, a sturdy waterproof windbreaker, good waterproof gloves, a warm toque, a variety of snacks, a water bottle, an emergency kit...

"I'm only going skiing, not mountain climbing," Thomas muttered. Still, he wasn't used to outdoor sports, let alone by himself. If he went out on a skidoo, it was with someone he knew; if he snow shoed, he was reluctant. Skiing was much easier because he could glide. It was like skating on top of the snow.

Last time he'd skied was during his last year of high school. It was a senior class activity to keep them all from drinking and being irresponsible teens. Not that *that* had worked.

He still remembered nearly breaking limbs racing down hills way too fast. Then there were make-out sessions behind the cabins when kids thought the supervising teacher wasn't looking. Most memorable, perhaps, was the heckling when any of them fell, even though they were all just as bad.

He wasn't sure he remembered all the basics. Thomas just hoped someone there would be able to at least tell him if he was screwing up too badly. He wanted a workout, so at least poor skiing technique would burn even more energy.

Thomas's mind wandered a little as he parked in the ski club lot. He stubbornly kept himself from thinking about the man who'd been on his mind for days now. Alex could be a real idiot sometimes, and not talking to him for a few days seemed to smarten him up most of the time.

Taking some space also kept Thomas's nerves cool. He hated losing control, even for a small outburst like snapping at Cam the other day. But that was another good reason to exercise a little more. Burn off the energy and frustration, and... hell, maybe he'd meet someone who caught his eye.

Maybe.

The actual rental took a few minutes of shuffling around on skis and trying out different pole lengths.

"I'm not sure I remember how," he admitted with a sheepish chuckle. "It's been years."

"Oh, you're doing just fine." The beardy young guy in hipster flannel plaid nodded as Thomas slowly scooted his feet back and forth. "It's just one foot in front of the other."

"What's the quietest trail? Seems busy today." Thomas had parked in the closer lot and that had been nearly filled. He'd probably nabbed that last parking spot from some early-morning skier who'd already come and gone.

"Probably one of the outer loops. A few people went up that way," the man gestured with a gloved hand. "I'd rather see you go on that trail since there's others out there in case you run into trouble. Nobody's been out the other way yet this morning."

Thomas appreciated his concern. "Thanks," he nodded. "I'll do that."

He set off slowly, not overeager to show off and fall on his face. He was glad he didn't embarrass himself before getting to the trailhead, at least. Once he slotted his skis into the tracks, he felt a little more stable. The ridges on the bottom of the skis helped him stay upright, but they couldn't do much. The tracks gave him an inflated sense of confidence.

He set off at a slow stride, his legs moving awkwardly at first in the strange shuffling movements. It took him several strides to find a good pace for his feet, and another several hundred feet for his poles.

It was a beautiful day, at least. It was warming up, some of the snow that warmed under direct light dropping off branches in clumps. It wasn't hot enough that the snow was wet and sticky, though; there was still an icy layer that made him glide along with relative ease.

This seemed way easier than Thomas remembered. As the cabin disappeared from sight and nature enveloped him, he pushed himself a little harder to get his heart pounding.

Peace, fresh air, and exercise: maybe this would be just the ticket.

Oh, fuck, he was sweating like a pig and his lungs burned with the cold air. His cheeks were so cold that he barely felt when his nose needed to be dabbed. Getting tissues out of his pocket was an elaborate exercise. He let go of his poles, wrested his hand from one of the straps, unzipped his pocket through thick gloves, finally got a tissue out and blew his nose, then reversed the whole process.

And he was drinking more water than ever. Despite being surrounded by the frozen stuff, he couldn't seem to drink enough. Plus, he'd already stopped for a few snacks.

He wanted to reach the cabin ahead – he just had no idea how far away it was. He finally came across a sign. *Another four kilometers?* Oh, fuck, he was never gonna make it back to the main cabin at this rate let alone another eight kilometers.

Thomas blew out a little sigh, wiping his forehead with his sleeve. He'd at least crest the next hill and emerge from the tree line. If he spotted the cabin ahead, maybe he could get to it.

He double-poled down the hill. In his exhaustion, he realized a little too late he'd misjudged the angle of the slope. It curved around a small hill and steepened almost immediately. By the time he saw the angle down, it was all he could do to try to bring his toes together. *Brake... I need brakes...!*

The adrenaline rushed to Thomas's head as he sucked his breath in. It was way too late to slow down. There weren't tracks on a hill this steep since it was safer to take the hill on the bare slope. They wouldn't have saved him, though.

"Oh, shit--"

Another skier was at the bottom of the hill. He was going to collide with him. He tried to skid sideways, turning like a downhill skier might to redirect himself. The move upset his precarious balance, and he didn't stand a chance against the slick icy surface and gravity together.

He tumbled hard, hitting the ground as his skis and poles immediately tangled.

"Shit, ow-- oof!" As he flipped into the deep snow and one arm caught in the trees. Then there was a *snap*.

Christ, don't let that be my arm or leg.

A second or two later he came to a stop, skidding around ninety degrees from where he'd gotten stuck in the tree. As the adrenaline faded just enough to become aware of his body, it was obvious that it hadn't been his own limb.

Thank god for that.

That left him with three main problems: that had been his ski pole snapping; he was a ridiculously long way away from the cabin; and the skier now just a few feet away looked horribly, impossibly familiar.

"Oh, god. It can't be." Thomas closed his eyes for a moment while his body shivered with the adrenaline coursing through him. Of course he'd have his near-death experience while *he* was right there.

But when he opened his eyes again, he shook his head. Thomas's eyes didn't lie. Even in a stylish white winter toque with a bobble on the top, the sexy man wearing that smirk had a smart mouth on him. He wasn't giving him a moment's rest.

"Taking the shortcut?"

"Fuck you, Alex." Thomas sneered for a moment, fighting to get his hands out from the ski pole straps. He yanked one out, then the other, and wrestled his skis free.

"I've never seen anyone fall that spectacularly. Are you okay?"

Alex smoothly sank to his knees sideways on the snow, not even tangling his skis in the process. He wore a look of concern that touched Thomas as much as it pissed him off.

"I'm fine," Thomas muttered, his emotions settling down. It was probably just as well he wasn't alone. If he *had* been injured alone, this would be a lot worse. "Just my pride... and that pole. Oh, man."

"It's a friggin' miracle you didn't break a leg. In downhill skis, you definitely would have."

"Thanks for that helpful commentary," Thomas snipped. He pushed his way back to his feet, his hands and knees sinking further into the snow. "There's a reason I don't go down hills on bikes, either."

Alex held back his clear urge to laugh and reached out a hand. Swallowing his pride for a moment, Thomas took the hand and Alex pulled him up to his feet. "The offer of mouth-to-mouth still stands," Alex teased.

"I wouldn't be caught dead kissing you." Thomas ignored Alex, stooping over carefully to grab one pole. He waddled up the hill a few paces for the broken pole.

"Do you want to borrow mine? They're taller since they're made for skate-skiing."

Thomas snorted. "Of course you don't ski like the rest of us plebes, either."

Alex looked startled, then laughed. "No, I – Thomas. I took lessons before. There's nothing wrong with the classic style. It can be very graceful and... speedy."

"Not the way I do it."

Alex laughed again. "Okay. Well, you're honest."

"No sense pretending I'm a star." Thomas hid his smile.

"I'll keep you company and make sure you don't break the other pole."

Despite his irritation, Thomas was surprisingly amenable to the idea. Somehow, the banter between them brightened him up more than if it had been some random stranger. "Okay. If you must. I was just heading back to the lodge anyway."

Alex nodded. "Me, too. I didn't know you skied." He pulled away and skated to the other side of the hill, then dug the edges of his skis into the snow in a V pattern to climb up the hill.

Still out of breath, almost dizzy from the adrenaline of the fall, Thomas followed. He had a harder time without being able to dig one of his poles in for support. He was clutching the broken pieces of the other pole in his left hand while trying to anchor himself with one pole.

It was a struggle, but he got to the top of the hill and scooted over into the tracks again.

"Do you want to swap skis?" Alex offered. "It might have to be boots too, though. I think we were the same shoe size..."

Thomas hadn't expected Alex to remember that detail. He hoped his warm cheeks were already flushed red from the cold air. "I, uh... nah. I'll manage."

"Okay. Let me know if you do."

He might have laughed earlier, but Alex was showing sweet concern now. Thomas's hackles settled as he set off in a slow, steady rhythm.

After a couple minutes, he had the best rhythm he could manage going. It was a bit like hobbling over the ice rather than the smooth glide he'd managed before, but it was something.

"What were you doing out here?" he asked Alex. "Working?"

Alex snorted. "I do take *a little* time off, you know," he grinned. "I often get home from work early."

"Really? I thought you'd be all... late nights."

"Nah. Not around here. A lot of the time, surveillance is best done in the early morning. Catching people going to work... stray pets are active in the dawn and dusk hours..."

"You find people's pets? Jeez, you're trying to be a good guy now," Thomas snorted.

"I'm trying. I know I've been a dick sometimes... am *still* a dick sometimes..."

Thomas nodded. "But I've seen a change in you already. Overall."

"Oh, yeah?" Alex brightened up. It was harder work for him to skate-ski slowly besides Thomas. It would have been easier to go fast and travel the distance with each glide, but he still did it effortlessly. He *did* have a pretty toned body, after all.

Oh, god, don't think of that here.

Thomas tried to think of some other topic of conversation, but none came to mind. He just stayed quiet for now, conserving his energy. Now and then, Alex caught his gaze.

This is nice. Just us, alone, quiet, not pushing each other's buttons... I could do this again.

The thought was as thrilling as it was scary.

CHAPTER
Sixteen

ALEX

IT WAS HARD NOT TO LAUGH AT POOR THOMAS'S EFFORTS TO ski. He looked like he hadn't been on skis for years, if ever, and he didn't quite know how to compensate with his other arm. He dragged himself along more than pushing, but Alex resisted the urge to critique his technique. That probably wasn't what he wanted just now.

After a few more minutes of quiet exertion, when they both slowed down for a drink of water, Alex looked at him. *Do or die.* This was the bit of trying to be a better person that was most uncomfortable. It never got easier. "I'm sorry I pissed you off the other day. I shouldn't have said those things..."

"That's half an apology, but I'll take it," Thomas snorted. "I shouldn't have hung up on you."

"No, that was cute," Alex teased. "I used to do that to you... a lot. Try to piss you off. God, I'm sorry for teenage me."

Thomas laughed now, the sound more relaxed and

genuine. "Yeah, but I liked the bad boys." He tilted his bottle back to down some water.

Mm, the outline of his throat bobbing as he swallowed... "You still like 'em?" Alex winked. Before Thomas answered, he added, "I know you're not looking to date me again or anything. I'm just flirting for the sake of it. If you wanna keep this... whatever we've had... to one hookup, that's fine."

Thomas looked startled as he tucked his water bottle in his jacket pocket and pulled his glove on again. "Oh. I see."

Jesus. Alex had almost forgotten... it was so hard to read him sometimes. "No, tell me what you really think. I've always admired you for having your boundaries, man. Nobody ever made you do shit if you didn't wanna do it," Alex told him. "It's something I'd look for in a boyfriend now, even though I got annoyed by it then."

"Would you look for a closeted boyfriend now?"

Alex glanced over sharply at Thomas. Was that a proposal or an honest question? He drew a breath, then let it out and nodded. "Yeah. I better get why some people do it now."

"What changed your mind?"

Alex set himself into motion, going as slow as possible while Thomas got up to speed. "Uh... working in security and investigation. I see a lot of unhappy couples and families. Chase, for example."

"Ah." Thomas cast a quick look at him. "You're looking for a boyfriend now? I didn't think you were the type to do boyfriends. You *barely* did when we were together."

"Believe it or not," Alex laughed. The squeak and rush of the snow beneath their skis was a beautiful backdrop to their conversation. Somehow, it soothed Alex's anxious nerves. "I went a couple years without dating guys for more than, what, two months?"

"That's not even a relationship, that's an extended fling."

Alex laughed. "Yeah, I know that now. But I dunno. Things are different since moving back here." He spoke carefully, not sure what Thomas was trying to coax out of him. His heart thrummed with nervous anticipation. "I just..." he trailed off.

No, don't say it.

If Thomas gave him an answer on whether he wanted a relationship again, Alex would tell him the gods-honest truth. He missed Thomas like hell and hookups with others weren't doing anything for him.

But he didn't want to push Thomas's comfort, and Thomas did seem uncomfortable. Alex wasn't sure if it was strictly at the idea of dating him, or men in general, but he was being awfully distant.

"Hm?"

"Nothing," Alex brightly answered. "I just saw a bird, I think."

"Oh, congratulations. You're a bird-spotter now?"

Alex laughed. "Smart-ass. It was a blue jay. It was cute. I'm not pointing out any more birds if you're just gonna make fun of me."

"No, point out the birds, please," Thomas groaned. "I'm sorry."

"Fine."

The mood was light between them as Thomas glanced at him. Those eyes were always perceptive. "If you were about to talk about us, I'm ready for that."

Alex's lips parted in a quick, small "O" shape – he knew his mouth was hanging open, and not just from exertion. His ski nearly slipped sideways as he lost concentration. He pulled it back toward his body and smoothly glided. "Oh.

Right. Um, I was just gonna say I really liked what we did the other night."

"Me, too," Thomas answered. "I thought it was one last fling, but it might be... the opposite."

Yes! Alex didn't even know why he was so excited at this admission. It wasn't like Thomas wanted to be his boyfriend instantly or anything. He didn't even know for sure he wanted Thomas to be!

But this was progress: for the first time, they were discussing their relationship like mature adults. And to Alex's surprise, it felt good.

There was nobody else in the main cabin – just the employees outside taking back the ski rentals. Once they ditched the skis and Thomas paid extra for his broken pole, they headed inside. They stripped off their ski jackets and pants to warm up for a few minutes before driving back home.

There were saunas and one outdoor hot tub, too. Alex was hardly prepared for Thomas in a swimsuit though – or even naked. He wasn't sure he wouldn't channel Darren and Anna's recklessness.

That last bit of evidence – video of them – was all he needed. Lexy would have her suspicions confirmed. Anna was more than a one-time fling. Darren wouldn't be able to talk his way out of it with the usual excuses.

Alex had to write up his report, but that could wait. Someone more important was here, sitting next to him on the bench in front of the wood stove.

Their knees grazed as Thomas stretched out, then placed a hand gently on Alex's knee.

A smile tugged at Alex's lips, and he turned his head to watch Thomas. He stretched his arm along the bench behind Thomas's back, then loosely wrapped it around his shoulders.

Logs crackled inside the glass-fronted fireplace as they watched the sparks fly and embers glow. The warmth was intense – almost unbearable – but Alex was hardly going to move.

"Would you drive back with me?" Thomas asked. "In convoy, of course. I want to talk somewhere private."

"Okay. Want to come over to my place?"

Thomas nodded. "Yeah. You'll have to lead, though. I don't know where it is."

"No problem." Alex couldn't look away from Thomas now. His cheeks were still flushed adorably red, his lips parted and wet and kissable.

Thomas's eyes had wandered down to his lips, too. He checked out around them, which Alex knew meant he was thinking about it.

"C'mon," Alex murmured. He leaned in to peck Thomas's lips and Thomas tilted his head so their lips perfectly met. After one sweet kiss, Alex pulled back. He rose, then offered a hand to Thomas to pull him to his feet for the second time that day.

Thomas took his hand and didn't let go as they walked down to the parking lot together.

Alex waited until Thomas was behind him before pulling out of the lot. His heart pounded with a kind of nervous excitement he hadn't felt in a long time.

He wasn't gloating at the possibility that Thomas wanted a repeat of the other day. Instead, he anticipated talking about their relationship. Hell, Alex worried that Thomas would slip away at an intersection instead of following him back to the city.

Something had changed in the way Alex looked at others – a new respect, perhaps. There was no more running from inconvenient situations; this time, Thomas had just as much power to break Alex's heart. And for the first time, Alex was okay with that vulnerability.

CHAPTER
Seventeen

THOMAS

"Come on in."

Thomas followed Alex into his apartment, shivers of anticipation already running down his spine. They were finally going to talk about what they were doing, and it was terrifying.

When he quizzed himself on why he was so worried, Thomas didn't like the answer he got. He was worried that Alex might not want the same things he did. Or, worse yet, that Alex *thought* he wanted those same things before he flaked out again.

But so far, they weren't letting go of each other so easily.

"Want a drink?"

"Water would be great, thanks," Thomas answered, crashing on the couch. He looked around Alex's little living room as he waited. It was plain, with a navy couch and a purple armchair providing a little color to the whitewashed walls. The huge bed in the corner had bright yellow and soft green blankets, like a little forest. That made him smile;

nature themes hadn't been Alex's style before, but it looked cozy.

Still, everything else was white or bare. There weren't even any photos up... no art or personal memories. Thomas frowned as he accepted the glass of water, and Alex sank into the couch next to him. "You're not putting down roots here."

"It's freaky when you do that," Alex snorted.

"Do what?"

"The uncomfortable truths. Please stop. I don't like evaluating myself and you're already making me do it in other ways." Alex winked.

Thomas laughed, nudging their knees together as he turned sideways to better face Alex. "Sorry."

"Yeah, like I said, I'm getting a house here in town. I didn't want to put in too much effort here before I move," Alex told him. He was jiggling his leg slightly, as if nervous. That was damn rare; his nerves were usually steady and hidden behind some professional expression.

He was nervous about talking to Thomas? Curious.

"So you're putting down roots *now?*" Thomas half-smiled. "You're not running away to the big city again?"

Alex scratched his throat and rubbed a thumb along his chin. He watched Thomas closely before picking up his own glass of water. "Like I said, my priorities are changing. I know I sort of... dumped you and ran, and that was a cowardly thing to do. But I'm not looking for the same things as I was back then."

"Hot sex and a guy who'd hold your hand in public?"

Alex hesitated before chuckling. He looked sheepish. "Actually, yeah, both of those things. But I want... more than that, too. What are *you* looking for? What have you decided on while I've been away?"

Thomas sipped from his water glass to stall answering. He had a pretty firm idea, as with everything in life, but he wasn't sure if it would send Alex running.

"A relationship. Something steady and long-term. I want to date a guy who's in this city for good, or at least for the next ten years. I don't want to be uprooting my life here to chase after someone just blowing through town."

Alex nodded slowly.

"And someone I like and trust, not just someone I have chemistry with."

"Do I meet those requirements?" Alex asked. His fingertips were white around the nails, like he was gripping his water glass hard.

Oh, fuck. He's... interested in my answer. And maybe me?

"You're serious?" Thomas asked, frowning. "This isn't just to try to... I don't know, make up for whatever we didn't do back then?"

Alex shook his head. "No. Since you moved here, I've been trying to decide if this is a good idea and damn it, I still don't know."

Thomas knew *that* feeling. He laughed and nodded. "Wait, you know when I moved."

"I... saw you around," Alex admitted, and this time, he blushed.

Thomas's eyebrows shot up. "You weren't surveilling me?"

"No!" Alex was quick to insist. "No, I honestly bumped into you at the barbecue. I was talking to Chase."

Oh. For some reason, Thomas had pictured Alex sitting in a van outside watching his every motion. That was a lot more mundane. Still... "Creeper," Thomas teased.

"Yeah," Alex chuckled and set aside his water glass. "Guess I never really got over you, eh?"

Thomas's heart squeezed, the air nearly sucked out of his lungs. Alex might well be joking, but this was the moment for him to be serious. "I never got over you, either."

Alex had stopped smiling, his eyes wide and gorgeous as they flickered between Thomas's. He parted his lips, drew breath, and paused. Then, he asked, "Really?"

"Yeah," Thomas nodded firmly. "I thought it was just because we never slept together before – but in bed the other night..." he trailed off. He wasn't sure how to explain that connection.

"I felt it, too," Alex said, his voice quiet. For once, there wasn't a hint of teasing.

"What have you been up to, really? Why are you suddenly so *for* relationships? Especially if you're all... biased against relationships from surveilling people and stuff?" Thomas asked. Alex was a bit of an enigma, and he had to figure him out.

"Ah." Alex half-smiled. "I slept around a lot for fun. And work, too."

Thomas nodded slowly. He could see that. Alex had always been an easy flirt, quick to reciprocate attention and perhaps a little too needy for it. And he was drop-dead gorgeous. All he had to do was turn on that charming smile.

It made Thomas want to irrationally dislike Alex more – perhaps out of jealousy – but he resisted the urge.

"I slept with a few people, I dated a few people," Thomas shook his head. "But nobody who... stuck on me like you."

"Yeah," Alex breathed out. "I know what you mean." He looked so relieved now that it made Thomas smile.

Alex's hand pressed against the back of his own. Thomas

turned his hand over to let Alex trail his fingers against his palm. The touch sent electric crackles of desire through Thomas's whole body.

Thomas laced his fingers with Alex's. He wanted to be more like Alex – a little more brash and brave, spontaneously daring...

He wasn't even sure if he was the first to lean in. They were suddenly kissing in a rush of breath and sliding lips, their hands rising to cup each other's cheeks.

The kiss was warm and sensual and familiar. He knew Alex's lips almost as well as his own. He knew that Alex loved having his lower lip sucked, and that sucking on his collarbone was the way to his dick. Alex got hard in just seconds of necking – inconvenient sometimes, but hot others.

Christ, perhaps more than moving back to this town, kissing Alex felt like coming home.

If it was a bad idea to sleep with your ex, why did this feel so damn *right*?

CHAPTER
Eighteen
ALEX

THOMAS WAS KISSING HIM HARD. ALEX FELT THE DESPERATION radiating through his body in waves of desire.

Holy shit, Thomas wanted him *bad*. Thomas was shifting to straddle him now, and Alex leaned back to let Thomas rest his weight on his lap. Not that there was much of it – he was a cute, scrawny thing, nothing like his brothers or Alex himself.

Alex kind of liked being able to lift him around, though. Thomas fit just right in his arms and under his chin these days. Besides, if he took up skiing, he'd get an even better ass. Though Thomas's was hard to improve upon.

"Mmm," Thomas groaned, snapping Alex back into the moment. Alex squeezed and rubbed that sexy little ass, then slapped it gently. Thomas tilted his head back to moan and catch his breath.

Alex leaned in to lick from the hollow at the base of his throat all the way up the vulnerable throat under his chin. Then, he kissed back to Thomas's mouth.

Thomas tilted his head, kissing him in return again. His

tongue plunged between Alex's lips, caressing the tip of Alex's tongue. He was barely breathing, his chest grinding against Alex's as his thighs slotted around Alex's hip.

Perhaps best of all, Thomas was grinding slowly against his thigh, his hard cock more and more obvious.

Alex was already *burning* to plunge inside that hot, tight body. He wanted to make Thomas moan and squirm and cry out with pleasure just like he had the other night. He wanted Thomas to come so hard he could barely manage Alex's name.

"Oh, fuck, yes," Thomas moaned, turning his head away again and kissing down Alex's neck. Alex let those soft lips kiss their way up to his earlobe, then shuddered.

He remembered *everything* about him. Including that little spot by his ear that made him quiver and pulse with pleasure... And the collarbone.

He pulled down the neck of his t-shirt with one finger to properly kiss and lick along the thin skin over the collarbone. Then, he nipped his shoulder and kissed along his chest through the t-shirt.

When Thomas reached under his t-shirt, Alex gladly stripped it off and tossed it aside. He worked at Thomas's t-shirt when Thomas reached up to let him. Once he was shirtless, Alex ran his hand down that bare chest to Thomas's stomach and over to his bulge.

Thomas bucked into his touch as Alex rubbed him through his jeans with the palm of his heel.

"I want you," Alex whispered, licking the side of Thomas's neck. He sucked for a moment, until Thomas quivered and his thighs clenched, then kissed over that spot. "I *really* want you."

"Me, too," Thomas moaned. His voice was a pitch higher,

his body half-melting against Alex as he looped his arms around his neck. He tried to sidle back as if to go off the couch on his knees.

Alex grabbed his shoulders. "Come to the bed first."

"Okay." They kissed as they stood up and they kissed as they walked over to the bed. Their hands never left each other for a moment, even when they fell onto the king-sized mattress. That was about the only thing in the apartment Alex cared about.

Oddly enough, he hadn't shared it with anyone since getting back. Even though he'd slept with a couple guys here – never satisfied with them, always yearning for more – he'd never invited a man back here.

That said it all.

He swallowed hard and rolled them over to kiss Thomas's chest.

"I was gonna suck you off," Thomas moaned. "But you're welcome to… get me started."

"I know. I saw you looking down there," Alex teased. He cupped Thomas's cheek until Thomas looked at him. Then, Alex kissed his lips a few times in little pecks until Thomas smiled. "I want to do it first. I… owe you a lot of apologies."

"Blowjobs as apologies?" Thomas laughed, but his eyes were sparkling. He looked playful again, not that painful mix of wary and half-hopeful emotions. Even those had been rare glimpses behind Thomas's brutally polite mask.

Alex murmured, "They never tasted so good…"

Thomas's thighs clenched and unclenched. His chest rose and fell rapidly for a few seconds as the words sank in.

"I've been *dying* for a taste of you," Alex whispered, pressing his lips firmly to the center of Thomas's chest. He kissed along to one of Thomas's nipples and sucked it gently, then dragged his tongue in a slow circle.

"Y-Yes..." Thomas moaned, his fingertips digging into Alex's shoulder. Thomas tried to wrap one leg around Alex's. "Please...!"

Alex chuckled deeply. "In time," he teased in a breathy whisper along the damp flesh.

Thomas's lips were open as he rolled his head back in a soundless reaction to that. Soundless? That wouldn't do.

Alex licked the other nipple, glowing with pride that Thomas already looked about ready to come on the spot. He had to wonder if Thomas burned with the same desire to touch and be touched every time they saw each other.

Alex kissed down to Thomas's stomach and around it, then near the waistband.

"Christ," Thomas whispered. "You're patient now."

Alex grinned. He liked taking his time to make his partner feel good, and when it was Thomas... Well, Thomas deserved the fucking *world*. He could at least give him a great blowjob.

"So worth it," he whispered. "Especially when you come and your face gets all scrunchy. You look like you've seen God. It's the hottest *and* cutest fuckin' thing..."

Thomas stared at him, his cheeks flushed with a mix of embarrassment and arousal. "I... Okay." For once, he was speechless.

Alex laughed and unzipped Thomas's jeans, then slowly wiggled them down his hips and off his legs before tossing them aside. Socks came off easily, too.

That left him in his underwear – sexy, tight boxer briefs that were bulging *hard* in the front.

Alex grinned and scooted back up the bed between

Thomas's legs, kissing his way along one almost hairless inner thigh. Thomas's body was so damn hot, and Alex had a feeling Thomas didn't even know it.

"Ah..." Thomas choked back a quiet sound when Alex reached his inner thigh without kissing his aching cock or balls. Just to make it even harder, Alex switched to the other thigh and pressed a slow series of kisses there...

"I'm gonna fuckin' kick you if you don't get to work," Thomas mumbled. Alex couldn't tell if it was a warning or a threat, but it made him laugh. He didn't remember the last time he'd laughed in bed and it had felt joyful and smooth, not awkward.

"Noted," Alex teased. He loved watching Thomas both helpless and on top of the world. There was something so damn visceral about sucking a man off, but it was ten times more intense with Thomas. He kissed over the bulge. It lay up and to the side now and lifted the underwear away from his body a little with how hard he was.

"W-We should've showered," Thomas muttered but Alex snorted. He didn't care about the extra bit of saltiness from his sweat on the trails; it was actually kind of fucking hot.

"Shut up and let me please you."

"Yes, *sir*," Thomas murmured sarcastically. He was gazing down his body and watching Alex like he'd never seen anything so hot.

Alex grinned. He hooked his thumbs in the waistband to drag his underwear down, admiring the pink, flushed length that popped free. "Oh, tasty." Thomas choked back a sound, but not in time. He *liked* Alex's dirty mouth. "I wanna see if it tastes as good as I remember," Alex whispered, kissing along the base. "It's so damn hot and hard already."

"Y-You've been fuckin' teasing me for five minutes now,"

Thomas almost snapped. His hips arched sharply off the bed at the first warm, wet contact. "Christ, if it weren't I'd be worried."

Alex smirked and licked from the base all the way up to the tip, watching Thomas's body go through a multitude of tiny shivers and shudders in response. Every muscle was clearly lighting up and quivering involuntarily as his whole body tautened with arousal.

Alex wanted to remember everything that pleased Thomas and show him that being with him could be great. He was memorizing every goddamn second of this encounter. He wanted to remember it for the next month in the shower at least.

And maybe longer. Maybe... much longer.

Alex hastily pushed back those thoughts. One thing at a time, and one thing demanded his attention. He closed his lips around the smooth tip, sucking his way down to the base of Thomas's cock in a smooth, steady motion. When he reached it, he pulled his head back up and sucked it down again.

It only took him a minute to get into a great rhythm – suck, lick, bob; suck, lick, bob...

Thomas's breathing was loud and harsh. The moans and whimpers that fell from his lips were music to Alex's ears.

"Yes..." Thomas whispered, then pushed on Alex's shoulder. "No, wait. You better stop."

Alex slowly pulled his head up off Thomas and grinned. "You want something else?"

Thomas nodded before he even finished the sentence. "Do I ever." He pulled Alex up, yanking him by his biceps in a surprisingly strong grip. When Alex was settled over his chest, Thomas kissed his lips, then swatted his hip. "You feel like you're about ready. Come on, you get naked too. No fair."

Alex was about ready to burst out of his jeans. The tight fabric was so damn painful, and he welcomed the chance to kick them off. He squirmed to get everything off, almost getting caught by his ankles before he was left naked.

"You want me to finger myself, or do you wanna do it?" Thomas grinned. "Either way, we're lubing up."

"Of course," Alex teased. "I'm doing it. Wouldn't miss the chance to tease you even more for the world..."

Now, Thomas groaned. "Oh, of course."

As Alex pressed his slick fingers to the opening, Thomas pushed into them and Alex leaned in to kiss him again. He loved sliding his fingers in to give Thomas a tease of what to expect next. Better yet, his fingers were flexible enough to get at all the *really* sensitive spots inside him.

He crooked his fingers until he felt the nut-like lump inside, then gently stroked his fingers across it. As his eyes flickered up to Thomas's face, Thomas's mouth fell open for another gasp.

"Oh, *fuck*, that's good."

Alex grinned. "Isn't it?" He rubbed a little harder, stroking his fingers along it. It was a treat to watch Thomas's body shiver and tense again, his stomach going taut as his cock twitched.

After another minute of breathy panting and wordlessly thrusting into Alex's fingers, Thomas's face cleared up. He braced his feet on the bed and swatted Alex's thigh. "You are *not* making me come already," Thomas informed him.

"Oh. All right," Alex nodded, his lower lip jutting out thoughtfully. "That's how it is."

"That's how it is."

It only took him a minute or two to finish getting ready, but Thomas already moaned to get him to hurry up. By the time he was pressing against and into Thomas, Alex was nearly losing control himself with his desire – no, *need* – for Thomas.

This time, he was going to do it right.

Alex slid in slowly, taking his time despite Thomas pushing into him forcefully. The enveloping, tight ring around his shaft never failed to feel good. It squeezed him to the brink of ecstasy all the way from top to bottom.

"Yes...!" Thomas moaned throatily. "Oh, yes..."

Alex grunted in agreement and leaned down, bracing himself on his forearm. The moment he could, he kissed Thomas hard. Their bodies thrust as if they were meant to be locked together in rough, raw pleasure. The chemistry was... well, incomparable.

Thomas kept mumbling and moaning encouragement through their kisses. His breathless words and begging were the hottest thing Alex could imagine. Even Alex groaned and grunted more than he usually would, his mind spinning with pleasure.

"You're so sensitive," Alex whispered, brushing his fingers along Thomas's nipple.

Thomas arced like he'd been zapped with electricity. He clenched around Alex's cock hard, interrupting his rhythm for a moment. "Alex!"

Alex drove in harder and faster. He whispered, "You're the hottest man I've ever known. You feel *perfect*."

"You're so fuckin' big, but I suppose you do, too," Thomas mumbled, smiling half-giddily as he said it.

Alex's eyes widened in shock before he kissed Thomas hard in punishment. "Asshole."

"Fuck me harder then."

"'Til you can't think up smart remarks?" Alex went deeper, guessing that was what Thomas wanted. Thomas's breathless sounds of approval confirmed it. Alex's whole body tingled, his fingers digging into the bed as his thighs clenched and his stomach drew tight. "Th-That'll never happen."

"You love it," Thomas smirked. Seeing that touch of an ego from the calm man was delightful.

Alex grinned. "I do." He reached down to run his palm along Thomas's cock. When Thomas grabbed his back, scratching up along his spine, he figured he was on the right track. He wanted Thomas to remember this forever, and he refused to think about why he might be so desperate for his approval.

"Yes...! Oh, I'm almost – Alex, I'm – Alex! Yes, please, Alex... just like that...!"

Alex could never forget how Thomas liked to be jerked off. A hard grip, his fingers acting as perfect ridges around the head of his cock, his thumb swiping around it now and then, an extra twist right at the end of each stroke...

Thomas clenched in pleasure, his muscles shaking as his eyes went hazy and lips parted soundlessly. Then he threw his head back and wetness was coursing out of his stiff, slick cock in quick, hard spurts of need. His body arched off the bed and his feet scrabbled against the blankets for a moment.

Alex was yanked down against Thomas's chest by how hard he grabbed and dug in his nails. Alex quickly ran his spare hand up Thomas's arm to pull it up and over his head. He pinned his hand on the bed above him, giving him something to grab.

Thomas squeezed *hard.* His face showed the most beautiful story of pleasure, written plain as day.

The extra tight squeezes, the sexy fucking sight of Thomas coming completely undone around and under him... it all added up. Alex felt his own orgasm hit a little too late to stop it and he gasped. He might have whispered Thomas's name or just thought it, he wasn't entirely sure.

Either way, he was driving hard into Thomas with each warm burst of pleasure that crashed through him. It was a fire deep in his belly and an electric crackle across every inch of his skin. It was a flush to his face and lips and the impossible need to be in Thomas forever.

Alex moaned wordlessly as Thomas let go of his back and cupped his cheek instead, hauling him in to kiss him.

Thomas didn't stop kissing him, either, as the last few drops trickled out. Alex had to pull out carefully before he softened. The only time Thomas let go was to let him throw out the condom. Then, Thomas was pulling him against him again and kissing.

Alex kissed back hard, trying to say it all with his body. Alex loved the way Thomas held him in this moment, like a precious thing. The deepest intimacy between them was in their eyes as Alex blinked to clear his head, then met Thomas, watching him like...

Well, like he loved him.

Alex's cheeks flushed with embarrassment. For a moment, he didn't know what to say. The idea was laughable: he'd quipped his way out of other men's beds all the time, but now Thomas watched him like he saw every thought behind his eyes...

It was almost disconcerting.

"Wow," Thomas whispered at last, and Alex laughed at

how that word really didn't cover it at all. Thomas quirked a brow. "What?"

"Just…" Alex trailed off, shaking his head wordlessly. He rolled onto his side, sliding his leg between Thomas's and running his hand down his side. He didn't care that his hand and Thomas's stomach were sticky as hell, or that he was gonna have to do laundry now. "It's strange." He hoped that word didn't sound wrong.

"It is," Thomas murmured. He understood what Alex meant: the strangeness of coming together again after all these years, almost as different people, but with the deep knowledge of each other before their adult defenses formed… after breaking each other's hearts in subtly different ways.

Christ. He had to stop psychoanalyzing himself. Thomas was rubbing off on him.

"Did you wanna stay the night?" Alex murmured, his heart fluttering with the impulsive offer. He had the feeling that might be moving too fast, but he had to put it out there.

Thomas's eyes flickered and he pushed himself up onto his elbow, then shook his head slowly. "I can't."

Can't or won't? Alex nodded anyway. "Fair enough." He lay back and let Thomas slowly gather his wits and get dressed.

Thomas moved jerkily, as if anxious about something. His eyes kept roving back to Alex. He smiled every time, but there was something else going on behind those deep eyes. Maybe he'd say what it was someday; maybe not.

"I'll walk you to my apartment door, at least," Alex murmured. He pushed himself up, surprised to find Thomas taking him by the hand for their short walk down the hall.

When they reached the front door, Thomas turned to

him and leaned in to press a quick kiss to his lips. "I'll see you soon."

That sounded like a promise – and a genuine one. Alex knew he'd lit up, but he couldn't play cool now. "Great. See you soon." He pecked Thomas's lips in return, then ran a hand over his shoulder affectionately before dropping it.

Thomas smiled back at him and let himself out as Alex watched. When the door was closed, Alex shook his head.

That was it, then. Whether Thomas was panicking about falling for his ex again or having to come out, Alex would have to deal with it and help him through it. There was no other choice, because Alex was stuck on this man.

CHAPTER
Nineteen

THOMAS

"YOU WANTED TO TALK TO ME?"

Thomas's palms were sweating, so he pressed them against his trousers before folding his hands behind his back. "If possible, yes," he addressed his boss with a polite nod.

Irma Davidson was a legend in the bank: she'd been working as a teller since she was fourteen, and all she'd say was that she was "considerably older" now. She looked past retirement age, but she clearly loved her work. She was the favorite of all the customers who knew her from years ago, and she was polite but firm with all the new hires.

Thomas had gotten on instantly with her, probably because she respected his work ethic. He didn't fiddle around on Facebook as much as the other young tellers, and he tried to see opportunities to jump in and help.

"Come on in." Irma invited Thomas into her office, holding open the door for him before crossing the room to sit behind her desk.

Thomas closed the door, then sat opposite her and folded

his hands. "I... wasn't sure about saying this, but I've been thinking about it, and..."

"All right, young man," Irma nodded, and Thomas's shoulders sank a little with relief. She wasn't rushing him. "What's going on?"

"I think I saw... inappropriate... conduct," was the best way Thomas could put it. "And it's by someone more senior, so I felt like it's tattling."

"No, I'm glad you reported this. When was this?"

"Last Thursday afternoon."

"What did you see?"

Thomas recited what he'd so carefully practiced: "I was walking by the offices to guide a customer back to his seat when I spotted, er... a blind ajar in Anna's office. I looked through. Not, you know, spying. Just accidentally. And Anna was... er, engaged with one of her clients."

"One of our mortgage clients?"

Thomas nodded. He'd watched the man walk out twenty minutes later looking cool as a cucumber, and he'd definitely spotted that wedding ring again. After a quick word with Maggie, he'd found out the rest of the story. He was Darren, he was supposedly sweet and charming, and Anna was helping him buy his first house with his wife, an adorable young IT pro.

"Do you know if this was one of her clients specifically?"

"Yes, it was. His name's Darren, but I don't know anything else except that he and his wife are her clients for their first mortgage. The ethics code..."

"I know what the ethics code says," Irma informed him tartly and he blushed. Her voice softened as she added, "Thank you for bringing this to my attention. I'll bring this to the proper channels. Anything else?"

"N-No, that's it." That was it? No interrogation? He'd been dreading having to repeat his story to all the managers, or being dragged into a room with Anna to tell her what he'd said, or... all the ridiculous situations his mind invented. "I felt bad about saying anything – it looks bad, and she's so good at what she does, but..."

"You did the right thing, kid," Irma told him in a voice that left no room for doubt. Sure, he doubted it internally, but he couldn't express it against that iron will. He just smiled sheepishly and stood up. "Thanks, Ms. Davidson."

"I wish you'd call me Irma," she answered, rising to her feet, but her eyes twinkled. She seemed to enjoy the formality; Thomas's peers called her by her first name easily, and he wanted to impress them. The bank was often a lot more formal than it appeared. Despite trying to look casual and hip to customers, there were a lot of people behind the scenes that were more impressed by cravats than the cool factor.

"I'll try to remember that," Thomas grinned back. He headed out of the office and back over to his desk, rearranging his pens and trying to focus on his everyday work again. It was early in the morning, and one never knew how busy the day would be. Monday usually was, though, as people came on their lunch breaks to finish the banking they'd wanted to do over the weekend when the banks were closed.

He'd be a terrible private investigator. He wasn't sure if knowing the secret or telling it had been worse, but what was done was done. That was the end of it.

It turned out that Thomas had only *hoped* that was the end of it. By mid-afternoon, it became clear that wasn't true.

A middle-aged man whom Thomas vaguely recognized from management – the central office, not the bank branch – asked to speak to him alone. Barry, he was pretty sure the guy's name was. *Gregson? Barry Gregson? Yes...*

The exchange drew the curious gazes of his coworkers. He shrugged to them and finished depositing checks and withdrawing cash for one of his clients. The clients came first, after all.

Minutes later, Thomas approached Mr. Gregson and was pulled into a meeting room.

"Good to see you again, Thom," Barry greeted with a friendly clap on the arm. It was a little old-boys-club and Thomas really didn't like the nickname, but he forced a smile and nodded. Where Irma came off as sincere and reassuring, there was something about this man he didn't like.

"Thanks, sir. You too."

"I've heard great things about you from Irma. In fact, I wanted to talk to you about your experience and education..."

Thomas hadn't expected that. He almost recoiled, then blinked and nodded. "Of course, sir. What did you want to know?"

"I understand your eventual career objective is to become a loan officer. If there were a position available today, with mentoring and training to help you transition roles, would you be interested?"

The direct question had Thomas flabbergasted. "I, uh... Um, yes, sir. I do want that. I just wasn't expecting to hear that."

"You've been turning heads for a while. I heard you went

to school in Halifax alongside your job to get extra skills, and I want to take advantage of that extra knowledge. It's wasted on the front end. We're looking to fill a position here as we transfer a loan officer to Halifax. You have a finance degree, right?"

Oh. This was the return of the boomerang he'd thrown out earlier today. He'd expected to be shunted away from well-paying promotions, not offered them on a platter. Certainly not offered the job of the person he'd tattled on earlier that morning. "I... I do, yes."

"And that's exactly what we're looking for.

"Ah, I see." Thomas fought his impulse to give an enthusiastic *yes*. "Um, what sort of timeline are you thinking for... giving me a chance to think about it?"

"I understand. It's a major promotion. Take a few days if you want, but we'd want to hear as soon as possible so we can fill that vacancy. I think you'd be well-suited to the job, and Irma agrees."

Alex swallowed. "Okay. Thanks, sir. I'd like to take some time to think about it, but I appreciate the offer." He'd always expected it to come from Irma, if it were coming from anyone.

"Of course. Let me know soon."

Barry came off less sincere the more Thomas talked to him, but Thomas shook hands anyway. He left the meeting room then, his mind spinning.

They were just transferring Anna to Halifax? Wasn't a breach of the ethics code serious enough to warrant firing? This guy was upper management, and Irma had never seemed particularly happy to have him around. Was this promotion offer even coming from her?

What the hell was he going to do?

The muffled clanging was a dull, comforting throbbing heartbeat in their backyards. Though the forge was muffled and the building insulated, the dull thudding was unmistakable.

Thomas loved it. He liked going out to help Jackson sometimes, collecting scraps or holding pieces down for him. He certainly wasn't built to be a blacksmith like his big brother, but it was a nice way to spend some time together. Sometimes they even had their manly bonding moments over a beer in the forge, or they could talk about whatever bothered them.

He'd talked Jackson through a bit of his feelings about dating Chase in that exact way. It only seemed right to approach Jackson with the dilemma of his own.

About the promotion first, not about dating Alex. He couldn't tell him about Alex...

Thomas knocked on the forge door and let himself in. "Hey, you busy?"

"Busy as I get," Jackson shrugged. "Always got time for you," he tossed a smile over at Thomas. "Come in."

Thomas grinned back and closed the door behind him, stomping the snow from his boots. Jackson really needed a walkway that ran from the house out to the yard. They had a back deck that stretched the span of all three properties so they never had to set foot on the ground as long as they shoveled it off, but not out here. Next summer, maybe.

"What's up?" Jackson followed up when Thomas didn't say anything. He unscrewed the clamped item – some kind of twisted rod – and gripped it in the tongs to dip back in the fire.

Thomas took a seat at the worktable nearby. "Not much. Just thinking about work."

"Yeah? More drama about missed lunch breaks?" Jackson teased. When Thomas took a moment to smile back, his eyes sharpened and he pulled the rod out, then clamped and twisted it. His eyes were more on the work than Thomas, but his attention was on his brother now. "Or deeper shit?"

"Deeper," Thomas admitted. "Would you take a promotion if it felt like a bribe?"

Jackson paused mid-twist, his brows furrowing as he looked up at Thomas. He considered the question, then shrugged. "It depends what the bribe's for."

"Tattling, I guess."

Jackson raised his eyebrow. "We're not in middle school. If you told someone about something serious, that's different from getting made a supervisor because you told them who breaks all the pencil tips."

Thomas managed a chuckle. "Um, it was a breach of the ethics code, more or less... I caught-- no, didn't catch, per se. Just happened to glimpse... one of the loan officers fucking their client. Their married client." Really, he was just as pissed at that Darren guy for being such a loser. *Bet nothing happens to him.*

Jackson raised his eyebrows. "You're talking... secret office illicit rendezvous? Jesus, have you walked onto a daytime soap?"

"Feels like it," Thomas laughed. "I told Irma, my boss – the cool one. Then this guy from upper management came to talk to me later and offered me a promotion to loan officer because they're moving her to Halifax. I really, really want and need the promotion, but..."

Jackson nearly dropped his tongs. "Wait, they're *transfer-*

ring her? Not firing her, or... disciplining her? Transferring to Halifax is a goddamn reward."

"I guess so. I don't know what happened behind the scenes. All I know is there was, um... internal stuff going on."

Jackson's eyes narrowed. "If that's the case, you probably weren't the only person to tell on them. Other people had to know."

That hadn't even occurred to Thomas. "...Oh."

"Upper management happening to be hanging around little old Fredericton? There was probably an internal investigation ongoing. They hire asshole private detectives like *that* guy to snoop around. You're probably just next in line for the promotion anyway."

Thomas opened his mouth for a moment, then closed it. *Ah, yes. I don't think he even knows I know Alex.* He cleared his throat. "I hadn't thought of that."

"Mr. Logical Dude hadn't thought that he wasn't the only fellow snooping?" Jackson grinned. "Office gossip is hot. I hear that's what people do all day. That and Facebook."

"Yeah. That's about right, actually." Thomas almost felt bad, but he knew Jackson made a hell of a lot more than he did for his extra physical labor. Well, at least a promotion would close that gap...

"I mean, cheaters are assholes and deserve to be dumped. If sleeping with your clients is prohibited – and I'd guess it would be for financial services like that – then yeah, you were right to tell," Jackson told him. "And don't feel bad if you decide to take the promotion. Needs must."

Only if I decide to date an asshole private detective? Thomas's cheeks were hot. "Yeah."

"Was that it?" Jackson looked perceptive as he watched Thomas. He turned his gaze back to his work, twisted once more, then laid the item on the forge to hammer it a few times this way and that.

"Um..."

Jackson glanced up. "Hey, you kept my secrets, I'll keep yours." Thomas hadn't told Cam when Jackson had chosen him over Cam to talk to about his new love interest. It was only fair that Jackson return that favor.

Thomas's cheeks were even hotter as he touched his face. "Yeah, uh. Just been weird, dating-wise. There's someone I've kind of... liked for a while now."

"Oho," Jackson grinned. "I knew that wasn't all." He set down his hammer and rolled his shoulders, leaning back against the table. "Spill."

"I'm still deciding if it's even a good idea."

"Why wouldn't it be?"

Really and truly, when Thomas searched his heart for the answer, he wasn't sure he had one that would stand up to scrutiny.

Alex had apologized for snooping on his family. Sure, he was a dick sometimes, but he was getting a lot better and Thomas could more than handle his smarmy moods. He seemed like he was here to stay this time. Hell, he rescued fuckin' stray animals.

More than that, Thomas hadn't stopped thinking about him since skiing on Saturday. When he'd gone to sleep Saturday night, he'd thought about sleeping in Alex's arms.

He was utterly hooked again.

"Just stupid reasons, I guess," Thomas admitted. "I don't know, you all seemed so certain when you chose people to date."

"Nah, it's not really easy from start to finish. It's a lot of scary figuring shit out," Jackson told him. "Whether you'll work together, whether you're both willing to work to stay together... There's so much to think about. The early stages are the worst."

"Yeah? Then why did you stick with it?"

Jackson's expression grew tender. He was a lot softer-hearted than most people realized, and he was shitty at hiding it behind a strong, silent mask. Seeing it happen – the switch in his entire mood when he thought about Chase – always made Thomas smile. "I just looked at him one day, once I realized he liked me as much as I liked him. And I... knew," Jackson admitted with a quiet laugh. "You know, can't stop thinking about him, want to protect him and be around him all the time, just... *want* to make it work, no matter what life throws at us. Or what barriers we each put up at first. You know, you want to push through all that."

Thomas felt like there was a lump in his throat. He hadn't expected *that* detailed an answer.

"Do you think this person would be the type to stick around and make it work? You need someone as stable as you are," Jackson told him.

Thomas half-smiled. It was odd, but he instantly knew the answer: yes. Alex was ready for more, and he was waiting for Thomas to say yes. Every sign pointed to it. Alex kept hinting that he would be okay if Thomas *didn't* want to get involved, and that he was interested in having a boyfriend, and that he liked spending time around Thomas again.

Until now, he'd instinctively thought it was the other way around. He'd just assumed he would always be pursuing, not pursued. What if it was *him* throwing up those barriers Jackson had just mentioned? Shit, what if he'd been doing that for years?

"Oh," Thomas murmured quietly. "Yeah, I... I think so."

"Then tell them and see what they say. They might just be waiting for you. You're an awesome guy," Jackson told him. "Let someone see that."

Thomas swiped an arm across his eyes and nodded. *If only you knew who it was. Oh, that's gonna be an interesting meeting. I'll put it off as long as I can.* "Thanks, man," Thomas nodded.

Jackson gave him a moment's genuine smile and reached out to punch his shoulder lightly, then yanked him in for a one-armed hug. "Now you've got my sweat on you."

"Gross!" Thomas laughed, shoving Jackson away and punching him harder, right in the chest. "God. Don't know why I offer to help you."

"I didn't know you were offering to help. Pick up those pieces," Jackson grinned. "I'll make something for you out of them sometime."

Little metal art pieces were already appearing in all three of their homes, especially as Jackson's work slowed down over the winter. Thomas wouldn't turn down another. He grumbled and shook his head as he gathered pieces.

Yeah, Jackson was pretty damn good at advice.

He had to call Alex... soon. Maybe tomorrow.

CHAPTER

Twenty

ALEX

Lexy was... devastated.

"I know it's not easy hearing this," Alex told her gently. "Or seeing it. I don't want to make you sit through it right now. Nothing – well, the last video, but almost nothing – is *incredibly* graphic, but it will be emotional for you."

"It's okay," Lexy whispered. "I'll believe you. What do they show?"

"All the other videos are what I already told you about." Alex pushed the DVD across the table to her, along with a small stack of written reports from the most important stakeouts. "The last one is from the ski trip I told you I was watching."

"And?"

"He and Anna... did... rendezvous in the cabin."

"Oh, god," Lexy whispered, pressing her fingers to her lips for a moment. "Do you think they're...?"

"What?" Alex frowned, but he spoke gently. She couldn't be pushed right now.

"Romantically involved?"

"It's impossible for an outsider to say, but... repeated meetings?" Alex shook his head. "That's not in the boundary of your relationship according to what you told me."

"I know, I know, but... I love him."

Alex went serious, a chill running down his spine. He reached out, letting her decide if she met him halfway. She did; her hands nestled in his larger ones. "Lexy, I mean this: if he's cheating over and over with different women, it's no different than over and over with the same woman. And this guy's doing *both*. You love *him*, but that'll never be enough. *He* has to decide to love *you*. If you two had decided to be non-monogamous? That would be totally different. But you didn't. You married him thinking you were the only one."

She was crying now, but quietly. It wasn't anything Alex hadn't seen a hundred times, but every time, it made his heart hurt.

This time, though, it didn't drive another nail into the coffin of relationships. Just *bad* relationships.

"I'll leave you with this until you call me again. This is far more than enough evidence for your divorce case, if you choose to take it that way. And this is completely personal advice, frankly, but... it's rare to find a man acting as badly as he is."

Lexy nodded slowly, pulling her hands back to grab tissues and compose herself. She sat up a little straighter. "Would you be there in court to present this?"

"If you need it, yes. If it goes that far. Most of the time it won't. When you show him the evidence, if you need me there for safety..."

"My friends will be there," she promised. "I'll be okay." She rose to her feet, gathering everything to tuck into her handbag. "I can't thank you enough. I'll pay your bill tonight when you send me the invoice."

"Okay," Alex murmured and rose to his feet. "Seriously, if you need my help with anything about this, call me. I don't want to see him win this one again."

"It's the last time," Lexy promised. Her voice was low, but determined. Alex had gotten through.

Despite worrying that he was going to be waiting weeks for his next call, Alex found himself almost annoyed by how many he was getting as soon as he turned on the TV.

He gave himself a reality check a second later. More business was what he wanted and needed. He'd leave the TV running all day if it made more people call.

But of course, when one call came in, he was guaranteed to get three. Just as Alex finished taking down the details of his next case, there was another call.

He hesitated, but he grumpily picked up the phone again.

"I don't know if you remember, but you asked me to give you a call if a MacLeod checked in coming from Ontario."

Alex sat bolt upright, muting the TV. "Yes, I did." Technically it was a violation of privacy laws to disclose the identities of guests in his motel, but George owed him a few favors. Also, George knew Alex wouldn't have asked him if he hadn't been serious.

"There's a fellow here by the name of Mark MacLeod from Ontario."

A chill ran down Alex's spine. He walked over to his wardrobe and yanked it open to grab work clothes. Professional enough not to attract attention, but clothes he didn't mind being ruined in a fight. "With a capital L?"

"Yeah. That was unusual enough, and I think you wanted to hear about a Mark..."

"I do. Thanks very much, George. I really appreciate this."

George answered, "You're welcome. Just don't get me into any trouble."

"Of course I won't. Thanks," Alex told him again, hanging up. He yanked off his sweatpants and hoodie, changing into his work clothes. He hesitated, his hand hovering over his private investigator ID. The province required that investigators carry it on the job, but he didn't necessarily want this being part of his work.

He swallowed hard and left it behind, grabbing his jacket and shoes. He almost tripped over himself in his haste to get out the door with his phone, wallet, and keys.

The bastard. How *dare* he?

The drive down to George's motel down on the river was quick. Alex took it about five over the speed limit – just slow enough that no cops would bother pulling him over. He really wanted to floor it, though.

He just hoped Mark was waiting before he went out for food, maybe resting up from the drive.

It didn't take Alex long to work out which motel room Mark was staying in. He parked around the side of the building in the guest spots, then found the car with the Ontario plates and obnoxious cross stickers. He strode to the door and knocked hard.

When the door opened, he almost recoiled from how familiar this man looked.

He was almost the picture of Jerry, Chase's ugly-ass uncle who had come to try to kick the gay out of him in August.

Alex would never stop feeling bad that it had been *him* that outed Chase's new identity and town after Chase had come here to flee his shitty family.

The least he could do was keep this new town safe for Chase.

"What are you doing here?" he snapped, pushing open the door further before Mark stopped him. "I think we need to talk."

"Jerry told me there might be a... *man* or two... in Charlie's life, keeping him isolated."

"Keeping him protected from assholes like you. You can get the fuck out of town. He doesn't want to talk to you," Alex told him flatly. Chase had driven Jerry out of town and told Alex to keep him out. He assumed that applied to other family members.

Even Chase's father.

"You have no right to tell me that he doesn't want to see me."

They'd gone in circles for a few minutes: Alex insisting flatly that Chase wanted him to stay away and threatening him as much as he could without technically breaking any laws; Mark insisting that he deserved to talk to his son because he was sad and missing his soul's salvation or some shit like that.

"Fine," Alex snapped. He was getting awfully sick of Chase's dad. "I'll go ask him, but I already know what his answer will be. When I come tell you it, will you fuck off?"

"That language isn't necessary. I want to speak with him."

"Yeah. Of course." Alex jerked his chin toward Mark. "You stay here. I'll be back soon."

He *hated* feeling like he was boxed in by his job. If he got a single assault charge, he'd lose his license. Anything that showed he was unstable or trying to bully his way around the job. The TV impression of P.I.s was a hell of a lot more sexy than the reality.

Alex breathed heavily as he climbed into the car, taking a moment to ground himself and calm down. He imagined the anger sinking out of him and through the bottom of the car into the ground. Then, he rolled his shoulders and started up the car. He knew a few quick tricks for getting himself mentally focused enough to safely drive after a tension-filled interaction. There were also other tricks, like how to escape aggressive dogs, but it had been a while since he'd had to do that.

The drive to the neighborhood where the three brothers lived was quick since Fredericton was pretty small. It was fast enough that Alex hadn't even fully formed what he wanted to say to the brothers. He just hoped he could see Chase without any of the others catching sight of him. They didn't have time to sort out the snarls of their relationships just now.

He did a few extra loops just to make damn sure he wasn't being followed. When he was certain it was safe, he pulled up in front of the trio of houses and parked on the curb.

Of course, the moment he stepped out into the snow bank, his feet sank through the crunchy icy layer on top into softer snow. Good thing he wore sturdy boots this time of year, though he grimaced anyway.

Wait. He smelled... burgers. In the winter air, the scent of a barbecue was pretty unmistakable. He couldn't really see any of the other neighbors being the type to barbecue in the winter. It also struck him as exactly the sort of thing these brothers would do.

Yeah, all of their cars were home, and the backyard lights were on. It was definitely them barbecuing, which probably meant they were all together.

"Oh, fuck," he whispered. But he didn't have a choice: he had to warn Chase and get his father out of town. He straightened up his shoulders, struggling out of the snow bank and onto the sidewalk.

Once he had his dignity again, Alex strode quickly up the walkway to Thomas's house first. If he were there, it would definitely be the best reception. Thomas could sneak off and grab Chase so as to avoid alarming the others.

After he rang the bell, there was no answer.

"That would be too easy."

Which of them was less likely to punch him: Jackson or Cam? No, more importantly, where were they more likely to be? He cast his mind back to the barbecue, then remembered seeing the less-weathered part of the porch where the grill normally sat. That was on Jackson's deck.

He strode up to Jackson's house to knock next, and sure enough, he heard voices a moment later.

Alex straightened up when the door opened, resisting the urge to wince. It was Cam, who would definitely recognize him.

Cam hesitated for a moment, his eyes narrowing in recognition and a quick search of his memory.

Alex nodded. "Hello. We've met before, but I need to talk to Chase now."

He glanced over Cam's shoulder to the quiet living room and... there was Thomas, frozen and gazing at him like a deer in the headlights.

Cam frowned suspiciously. "Chase? Why? You're... You're that guy from the park, aren't you? The hockey court? Who looked for me?"

He *could* use his relationship with Thomas to get inside, but... that would be a dick move. He just smiled and nodded slightly. "I apologize for that. I know you're probably pissed off, but I wouldn't be here if I didn't need to talk to Chase."

Jackson was walking up now, scowling. "This is the guy who looked you up?" he asked Cam. The two of them blocked the doorway while Noah and Thomas stayed in the background. He couldn't see Chase yet. "You're not the same detective who tracked down Chase?"

Well, this isn't going well. Alex nodded again. "And I've done all I can to make up for that. That's why I'm here now."

Cam looked at Jackson, deferring to his judgment.

Jackson paused, then nodded once. "Come on in."

The atmosphere was far from friendly as Alex stepped into the second Riley brother's house. He'd never been into Cam's, but hopefully he wouldn't have to see it anytime soon if this was any indication of his reception.

Alex resisted the urge to catch Thomas's eyes. He didn't want Thomas to intervene and out himself, after all. He could handle an ice-cold reception from Cam or a hot-tempered guy like Jackson relatively easily. And Noah was watching him with a fair amount of resentment, but he didn't pose a huge threat either. Thomas just had to stay quiet and nobody would have to know.

His heart squeezed as he wondered how long Thomas would stay silent, or if this would be the finishing straw. Maybe Thomas saw how hard it would be for him to integrate into the family. He could pick pretty much any guy he wanted and they'd be quicker to accept him.

"So... where's Chase?"

Jackson eyed him again, then nodded upstairs. "Just up there. He'll be down in a minute."

Alex folded his hands behind his back and stood straight, offering a polite smile. This wasn't how he'd pictured his first meeting with the family of his lover, but... needs must.

"Is he in danger?" That was Jackson, his annoyance fading into concern for his boyfriend.

Alex drew a breath and let it out, then nodded. "Only a bit. I can deal with it. I just need permission."

Jackson licked his lips, clearly screwing up his pride, then gestured at the couch. "Come on, have a seat."

Though he'd almost prefer to be standing, Alex smiled and accepted the invitation, sinking onto the couch. He tried to prepare for the questions he knew were coming.

All he focused on, though, was Thomas sitting on the other end of the couch.

He finally let his eyes flicker over to Thomas and nodded slightly, then looked over at Jackson and Cam as they sat opposite him. Noah sat on the arm of Cam's chair.

Jackson raised his voice. "Chase!"

Thomas flinched. His nerves were possibly more wound up than either of his brothers', then.

"Someone to see you."

Jackson turned his gaze back to Alex, his expression shifting. He'd let go of the grudge already, focusing instead on the current crisis like Alex wanted him to do.

Good man. I can work with him.

Hopefully the rest of them would be the same.

WHEN THE DOORBELL RANG, THOMAS HADN'T IMAGINED WHO it would be. He'd certainly never imagined Alex being invited inside by his protective older brothers. Though... he *had* imagined that if they ever met, it would be about this awkward.

Christ, they were all stiff and tense. It was like bulls in the living room. Noah was about the only one looking less tense than everyone else.

Once Jackson called out to let Chase know he needed to come downstairs, silence settled for a few seconds. Then, Cam spoke up.

"How have you been, then? I think you were in my class."

"I was, yeah," Alex nodded. "Been good. Lived in down-town Toronto for a while, traveled around... I like being back, though."

"Yeah. Coming home is always weird, but it's all right here."

Thomas dared to let out his breath. Cam seemed to be

making an effort. Now that Jackson was focused on Chase's well being and not what Alex had done to him before, the atmosphere was settling. The only wild card was Noah, who was usually pretty easy to read but was on his guard now. Knowing him, he was probably still irked but politely hiding it.

Chase came down a minute later, having changed out of his barbecue sauce-stained shirt and washed up after the tremendous accident. Cam had been gesturing too enthusiastically and slammed his hand on a bottle of sauce that was lying on its side but open. It had squirted in Chase's face and over his shirt.

The uproarious laughter from minutes ago was all but forgotten as Chase froze on the stairs. "Oh. It's you."

Alex looked wryly resigned to the less than warm welcome as he rose to his feet. "I don't want to be blunt, but there probably isn't much time. Your father's in town. I need to make sure you don't want him around."

"Of course I don't," Chase scoffed, his eyes narrowing and shoulders tensing. "Is my uncle there too? Or did Dad come alone?"

"Just your dad."

Thomas swallowed, glancing between them.

"Well, we can go fuckin' sort this out, then," Jackson said. He rose to his feet before Cam grabbed him and pulled him back into his seat.

"No, we should let Alex deal with it. The less they know about us, the better," Cam told him. "And you don't need to be getting in trouble."

Chase was silent, his eyes flickering between them all.

"He should be seen out one way or another," Jackson argued.

Cam nodded. "Yeah, but not with a fight. The cops arrest you and it looks bad on everyone."

"They don't have to arrest me."

Chase took the last few steps down the stairs and approached. "Guys--"

Noah spoke up. "You really think he's the type not to call the cops? He has a vendetta against you now, remember? We can't threaten or intimidate them."

"Religious wackos," Jackson scoffed. "So what?"

"Let Chase decide what he wants to do." Thomas spoke up louder, nodding at Chase. Chase had been looking like he wanted to say something.

"How do we know this is the truth?" Jackson frowned, looking over at Cam and then Alex. "That his dad's really here? Maybe it's some other MacLeod."

"Obviously you don't, but Chase told me to let him know if anyone came back to town. I've been watching ever since. I talked to him in person – I know it's him."

Jackson sucked in his breath. "You went to confront him? Why? Why isn't he gone yet?" His tone was slightly accusatory. Chase came over to stand by him, rubbing his back slightly to bring him back down.

Alex stayed calm, not rising to the bait. "I wanted to deal with it immediately, but he wouldn't leave without hearing directly from Chase that Chase doesn't want to talk to him."

"So, what, Chase goes to talk to him? Hell, no," Jackson scowled.

Cam shook his head. "Not by himself. With one of us? Or all of us..."

Noah laughed under his breath. "Back to the threats," he commented, though they ignored him. Thomas thought he was right, though: calm conversation was better than overreacting. The more they reacted, the more likely the whole family would show up on Chase's doorstep to try to free him from them.

"I'm going with him," Alex told them firmly. "But I don't think any of you should come."

There was a resounding moment of silence. Thomas knew exactly what Alex's logic was, but he winced anyway. *Oh, this is going to go well.*

"I want to be there," Jackson immediately disagreed.

"No." Alex gave him a long, steady look. "There's too much risk you'll lose your temper at him and I can't be involved in violence. This is a calm meeting where we tell him to fuck off or we get a restraining order."

Jackson still narrowed his eyes. He didn't look happy with that answer. "Can we trust you to keep him safe? I don't know you from Dick," Jackson scoffed. "I don't know you're not just acting under his father's orders again. You fucked up Chase's life and Cam's."

Alex opened his mouth to retort, losing his cool for the first time as heat flushed to his cheeks. "Not because I didn't do my job. I'm trying to do it, if you'd let me--"

Thomas rose to his feet. "Stop it," he snapped loudly enough that everyone listened. "Jackson, even you. I know you're worried for Chase, but you can trust Alex."

Jackson was startled out of his annoyance, his shoulders sinking again. "How do you know?"

"Because *I'd* trust him with anything." For a moment, Thomas understood what Cam might have felt that spring. He wasn't fainting, but fuck, it almost felt like it. His fingers tingled as nervous heat flushed through him. His heartbeat raced in his stomach.

"Fuck it, let's go. I'm going with you," Thomas told Alex.

Alex knew better than to disagree. He nodded slightly. Thomas strode for the back door, shoved his boots on, and headed out along the back porch to get his jacket from his own house.

The air hit his lungs with the bitter cold of a January evening. He almost felt like he couldn't breathe now, but steam hung in the air from his heavy breath so he knew he was fine.

He'd probably just come out to them.

Christ, it was about time, though.

Thomas grabbed his jacket from his own house and zipped it up, then took the shortcut back to Jackson's house again.

Chase was in his winter jacket now, his boots on. Alex stood by the door while the other three men stood nearby. This time, they weren't crowding him though.

"All right," Thomas said. "Let's go sort this shit out." He didn't wait to look at Jackson, Cam, and Noah, though he felt all three of them watching him. His cheeks still burning, his hands almost shaking as he pulled open the door and stepped onto the porch, followed by Chase.

"Brr," Chase whispered, shoving his hands into his pockets. "God, it's cold."

Thomas was too busy listening behind him.

"Bring Chase back safe and sound," Jackson said to Alex, his voice low. "If my brother trusts you, that's enough for me... but..."

"I understand," Alex instantly assured him. Thomas glanced back in time to see him grab Jackson's hand and shake it once. "We'll be back soon."

"Okay." Jackson let out a breath, then reached out to pull Chase in for a quick, crushingly tight hug and kiss.

Thomas accompanied Alex down to his car, giving Chase the front seat while he sat in the back. He glanced out the window, watching scenery pass by as he settled back.

We'll deal with it later. First, we get Chase's situation sorted out. Thomas had waited long enough... a little longer wouldn't kill him.

Twenty-Two

CAM

Even after bringing the food in to keep it warm in the oven, Jackson had too much energy to sit still. He was pacing around the kitchen and living room, taking every opportunity to stand up to fetch another beer or tidy something up.

His restlessness made Cam twitch, though Noah was doing his best to rub his shoulder and clap Jackson's arm, keeping them more or less grounded.

None of them said much at first. It probably took the others a couple minutes to process the encounter with Alex.

For his part, Cam's mind raced. Thomas had sounded so familiar with Alex – his defense of him hadn't been reasoned, but impassioned. That much directness was rare for him.

"So, I wonder what Alex is doing around," Cam finally said. There was no point in pretending it wasn't what was on all of their minds.

"Chase *did* ask him to keep an eye out for his family," Noah murmured. "We talked once or twice about... that kind of stuff."

"Oh?" Jackson looked at him, and there was no hiding the hurt expression. "He never mentioned..."

"Probably didn't want you to get... like you get," Cam laughed. When his older brother gave him a rueful look, he smiled. "Not that I'm blaming you. If Noah were in that situation, there'd be no stopping me either."

"I still can't believe it's the same guy who fucked up Chase's life *and* yours."

"He didn't actually do anything--"

Jackson scoffed. "He made you almost have a heart attack."

That was *sort* of true, but it was a bit of a stretch. Cam didn't want to push any buttons while Jackson was understandably worked up, though, so he just shrugged. "I just didn't know it was the same guy."

"I'm more worried about Thomas," Noah murmured, rubbing his chin. "I didn't know he and Alex..."

"Yeah, what was that about?" Jackson frowned. "He talked to me the other day about some kind of promotion he was offered as a bribe. He said he found this inappropriate work situation, but... what if Alex is involved? God, I hope he wasn't the one investigating on the company's behalf... using Thomas for information or something."

Cam leaned back on the couch and kicked his feet up on the coffee table. "It's possible," he admitted. "I don't think he seems like that kinda guy, but it is. I don't remember much about him from school, just that he was kind of a... I don't know, bad boy. And he wasn't quite *out*, but everyone knew. He didn't talk to you or me much, did he?"

"Yeah," Jackson hummed. "I barely remember him. He would've only been getting into high school when I was leaving anyway."

"What if they dated?" Noah asked, his voice carefully neutral.

Jackson scowled. "I knew there was something weird when I mentioned detectives and stuff... If he's another ex like yours..."

Cam chuckled quietly. His asshole ex, Nathan, had tried to call him twice after he'd gotten together with Noah. He'd ignored both calls and blocked his number not long afterward under Jackson's advice, but it hadn't really been necessary. He just didn't give a crap about the guy anymore. He'd stopped caring after meeting Noah.

God, Noah had changed everything for him.

What if Alex could be that guy for Thomas? Nah, it seemed ridiculous from even the little they knew of him.

"I hope he's not trying to screw with Thomas now. Thomas always hid everything from us, and... he did say there was someone..."

Cam's stomach twisted. Sure, he didn't care about Nathan now, but it had taken him a long time to get to that point and multiple breakups with him. Exes might be Thomas's weak spot and they'd never know. "If he's getting him into trouble at work we'll find out and figure it out."

Noah sighed. "You two are being a little defensive."

Cam blinked and looked at him. He wasn't expecting his own boyfriend to chide him, even if his tone was gentle.

"You're charging in like bulls in a china shop. Thomas is only barely talking to us. If something *is* wrong with this Alex, he'll tell us now that we know about the two of them – unless you scare him off."

Jackson was nodding; he saw as well as Cam where this was going.

"And if he *isn't* as much of an asshole as we think from

our very limited exposure to him, well," Noah flourished his hand. "So much the better. Romance at last."

Romance? Ridiculous.

"Wait," Cam whispered, sitting up straighter. "No, wait. Alex studied with Thomas before. I forgot 'til now, but... he mentioned an Alex. He only talked about hanging out a couple times, but... there *was* an Alex. If it's the same one..."

"There are only a dozen Alexes in each graduating class," Jackson muttered.

Cam shook his head. Something told him that his intuition wasn't wrong. The way they'd watched each other in those fleeting seconds... It was like there was a mutual secret.

"I think they were dating... or they are now. Could've been unrequited back then, who knows?" Jackson frowned. "But yeah, Noah, you're probably right. Unfortunately."

Noah laughed. "Cam says that a lot, too," he winked.

Cam pulled Noah onto his lap and slipped an arm around his waist, squeezing him in a quick hug. "Thanks for the voice of reason."

"You're welcome."

"God, I want a beer," Jackson snorted. "Anyone else?"

Cam frowned. He'd had one earlier and he was limiting himself to a single drink no more than three times a week until he cut down on his beta blockers. "Not 'til the doctors say so. Maybe pop, if you're going for one."

"Hey, but look up," Noah smiled, twisting sideways to see Cam's face. "That was pretty stressful and you didn't even look dizzy."

Oh, yeah. Cam slowly smiled back and shook his head. "I wasn't." Before surgery, he would have had to at least sit down for a bit afterward and get his heart rate down. At worst, he might have passed out right in front of Alex.

"That's good news," Noah smiled and kissed him. He stood up to grab a beer for Jackson and pop for himself and Cam.

Cam exchanged looks with Jackson, who at least looked calmer than he did earlier. The stress on his face over what was going on with Chase right now still showed, though.

"They'll be back any time now," Cam assured his older brother. "If not Alex, Thomas will make sure of that."

Jackson relaxed a little more and nodded. "Any time now," he agreed, taking his beer from Noah before Noah settled on the arm of Cam's chair again. "And cheers to another successful heart test."

They raised their drinks to that, then settled back to wait.

Twenty~Three

ALEX

It wasn't hard to feel the awkward silence in the car. With Chase in the front seat and Thomas behind him, Alex didn't especially want to start polite conversation. Chase had other things to worry about, after all.

"Where's he staying?" Chase finally asked as they waited at a light.

"The motel on the river."

"Oh, that tacky old one?"

Alex half-smiled. *Don't tell George that.* "Yeah."

"Eugh," Chase muttered. He turned to glance at Thomas, then looked at Alex; it was easy to tell what he was thinking. "You two know each other then."

Alex's gaze flickered to the rear-view mirror. He just nodded, focusing on pulling out into traffic again.

"We dated in high school," Thomas said.

Alex's foot nearly slipped off the gas pedal. *Holy Christ.* To his knowledge, this was the first time Thomas had ever told anyone else that they were dating or had dated. And it wasn't even his own brother he'd just told.

He adjusted his heel and checked his mirrors, licking his lips.

"Oh, right," Chase answered, glancing between them again. "I didn't know that, sorry." The clear implication was *do your brothers know?*

"No reason you should. Nobody else knew," Thomas chuckled quietly.

"Ah."

After a few moments, Chase looked at Alex again. "And you... investigated Cam, too? I couldn't really make out what that was about."

"Er, yeah." Alex chuckled awkwardly. "I took a case where I was investigating whether he was moving back here to play hockey for the new minor league team instead of quitting, as the media had been told."

"Oh."

"For the record," Alex said, glancing briefly at Thomas, "I told them he was out. It was my professional opinion his amateur league was for fun and that he really was disabled."

Thomas nodded slightly.

"But they didn't believe that," he explained to Chase. "I arranged a meeting, and from what I heard Cam... fainted afterward, so Cam and Noah hold me at fault for that. Which I can't completely disagree with."

"So you investigate disability claims?" Chase asked. "That's what all that was about?"

"More or less. Since then, I've stopped taking those cases. They're very lucrative, but... there's so much potential to make a wrong call. I could say he was able-bodied because he was playing in that league if I were working for his insurer, even though he was pushing his limits to do so. I would never know that. I might say someone's fine when they're using the last of their strength to go out and do errands..."

"Ahh," Chase murmured awkwardly. "Wow, I never realized that. They really hire people to check them out?"

"Not every claim, but yeah, a lot of them. I think... some of them are denied for pretty bullshit reasons now that I know both sides of it," Alex admitted. "They only prosecute for fraud in extreme cases and I've never been involved with anything that wasn't a clear fraud, but... there's always that potential." He felt Thomas quietly watching from the back-seat and cleared his throat. "Almost there."

"At the motel?"

"Yep. Anything you want me to do or not do?" Alex asked, his hands tightening on the wheel. "Thomas or Chase?"

"It's not my bone to pick," Thomas told him. "Chase?"

Chase looked hesitant. "Not... exactly. I just don't want them around. That's all. No matter what he tries to manipulate me with."

Alex nodded and shut off the car as he pulled into the guest parking space. He reached out to rest a hand lightly on Chase's shoulder.

Chase seemed surprised, then grateful as he glanced over to Alex. "You don't *have* to come in..."

"I really don't mind," Alex assured him quietly. It wasn't the worst he'd ever seen, and he really fucking hated the idea that he'd ever led Chase's family to find him. Given his time back, he never would have taken that job either.

Jesus, he was gonna be out of work soon if he kept avoiding cases.

Chase nodded, steeled himself, and climbed out of the car. As soon as he did, Alex and Thomas climbed out of the other side and Alex exchanged looks with Thomas. "Nothing threatening or dangerous," Alex warned him quietly. "Do you really want to come with? You can wait here."

"I'm coming," Thomas told him firmly, but he brushed his hand lightly down Alex's arm.

Alex accompanied the men around the side of the building to the motel room Chase's dad was staying in. "I don't know for sure he isn't armed," Alex warned them. "I did a quick check earlier while I was here and I didn't see any signs, but... Has he ever used or owned weapons, Chase?"

"No. No, nothing," Chase shook his head. "I'm... I'm sure he wouldn't..." he trailed off. The hesitance that crept in at the end of his sentence made even Alex's nerves spark with anger. "I don't think he'd be dangerous."

"Okay," Alex told him calmly. "But let me stay closer to him first."

When Chase nodded, Alex knocked on the motel room door.

Mark opened it seconds later, scanning Alex's face with a grimace of displeasure before his gaze landed on Chase's face. His whole expression warmed up, but Alex saw through it to the underlying emotions. It was safe to say the other two did, too.

"My boy. Come on in."

"I don't need to come in," Chase told him flatly. "I just need to stand here and tell you I don't want to see you again, unless you've come to apologize."

"Charlie, I came to talk to you about--"

"You *start* with the apology if you're here with one," Alex told him sharply. "And his name is Chase now."

"*Charlie,* I'd happily speak to you in private," Mark emphasized, clearly trying to ignore Alex.

Chase scoffed. "You talk to me here or never."

Mark seemed taken aback by his son's attitude. He scanned Chase's face as if looking for something he recognized.

"I told Uncle Jerry the same thing. I want nothing to do with any of you, even if you *were* to apologize. You screamed about the devil to me and made life a living hell in the meantime."

"But your brother – Luke misses you."

Alex shook his head and interrupted again. "You can't impose conditions on this if you're offering a chance for Chase to see him again." It was painful to see the hope in Chase's eyes. "You accept Chase as a visitor for Luke the way he is or there's no deal."

His chest quickly rising and falling, Chase nodded and looked back at his father. "What he said. I'm not going to hide who I am to see Luke."

Mark scowled and shook his head. His expression was ugly now, that false smile gone already. "I can't let you influence him like *that*."

"Then here's the final answer, and you can tell this to *everyone* in the family, like I told Uncle Jerry to," Chase said, his voice hard again. That hope gone from his eyes, all civility was gone from his voice now, too. "No-strings-attached contact with Luke and a sincere apology from all of you. Until then, you don't contact me or look me up in any way."

Alex was blown away by how clearly and forcefully Chase spoke. He'd been in a few stand-offs between spouses, family members, and even bosses and employees. Not many victims confronted their past so eloquently with almost no warning.

"And if you do contact him again without following those

conditions, I'll help him get a restraining order," Alex told him. "You know what I do. I know the process *very* well."

Mark shook his head. "I guess he was right about you." The disappointment in his voice was such a transparent attempt to manipulate Chase that Alex laughed. "You're beyond hope."

"I'm the fag you never wanted," Chase agreed with a bright smile. "And I love it."

Mark's eyes flickered between Thomas and Chase. Thomas was pretty easy for anyone to pick out as gay – or so Alex thought. There was no doubt Mark thought they were involved now. "You two? You're not the one Jerry told me about," he glared at Thomas.

Thomas looked taken aback. "A man can be gay without fucking everyone around him. Rude. I'm involved with Alex, actually. Not that it's any of *your* business."

Alex restrained his laughter at Thomas's sudden bad language. He stored away his moment of joy at Thomas's bluff... or, perhaps, not even a bluff. "We're going now. If any of you change your mind, call me first. If you show up in town again, we'll take legal action. C'mon."

Mark was silent, but his knuckles were white as he gripped the edge of the door. It was almost disconcerting the way he watched the three of them walk to the car.

Just before they rounded the corner, Alex glanced back and saw it: the fight went out of Chase's father. His hand slid down the door to rest on the door handle instead, his shoulders slumping. Then, he leaned against the door to close it.

Chase won.

Alex didn't say anything until they reached the car.

"You get in the front," Chase encouraged Thomas.

"You sure? I can sit back here with you--"

Chase laughed quietly and half-hugged him. "I don't need to be minded," he assured him simply. "I'm not shedding any tears over people who aren't worth it. Sit up front with the man you're involved with."

Thomas blushed at the teasing. He almost slipped on ice in his haste to get into the passenger seat.

Alex grinned at Chase, then waited for him to get in before climbing in and starting up the car. With any luck, the drive back would be a lot less awkward.

His heart was warm at the protectiveness Thomas showed toward Chase, though. And earlier, even though Chase wasn't their blood relative or even boyfriend, Cam and Noah had been protective of him. Jackson, of course, had been like a bear sheltering his cub.

More than anything, Alex wanted to feel that kind of warmth and bond. Would the Rileys ever let him in?

Twenty-Four

THOMAS

"Was it your guilty conscience?"

Thomas's jaw dropped as he twisted in his seat to look at Chase, then at Alex.

Even Alex seemed startled at Chase's direct question. "Wait, what?"

"That made you... want to help me out like this," Chase said.

Alex glanced over at Thomas, his lips quirking up. "Well, he doesn't beat around the bush, does he?" He looked in the rear-view mirror for a moment, keeping his eyes mostly on the road. "I suppose at first, yeah."

"At first?" Chase looked curious, not accusatory.

Alex nodded, rubbing the wheel with his thumb. "Yeah. I felt bad about putting you in danger from them again. But now... I'm genuinely interested in you... especially 'cause you're Thomas's family."

Oh. A little shiver ran down Thomas's spine as he watched Alex speak.

"I want to help them out, and..." Alex trailed off.

He slowed the car down as he approached a line of waiting cars at a light. At last, Alex's eyes flickered over to Thomas. His hand rested on the gear shift, his thumb tapping the stick with a subtle hint of nervousness.

Wisely, Chase didn't interrupt the moment. He busied himself looking out the window.

Thomas licked his lips, then reached over to rest his hand on Alex's. He wordlessly smiled.

Alex relaxed again and smiled back. The light turned green and he kept his hand on the shift as he pulled away again.

At last, as they pulled into the Rileys' neighborhood, Thomas spoke up again. "Thank you for helping. That was really... really appreciated."

"No problem," Alex said softly. "Glad to help out."

"Did you mean it, about the restraining order?"

Alex nodded. "I can help you, if it comes to it." His grip on the shift tightened as they turned an icy corner, then relaxed again. "But don't worry about that yet. It's a long way to go before that happens. I don't think your dad will be back in town any time soon."

Thomas hoped he was right. Alex had seemed authoritative and a little intimidating without actually uttering any threats. Come to think of it, he'd defused the situation perfectly. How much experience did he have with that? The thought of Alex standing off against assholes like that Mark without backing down...

It was a little hot, actually.

Thomas cleared his throat, then unbuckled as Alex parked by the curb.

The front door was already open, all three men in the doorway as they clambered out of the car and onto the snowy road with the crunch and squeak of boots. Their breath hung thick in the air, the temperature having dropped even further.

Chase led the way back to the house and Jackson pushed past Cam and Noah to step out onto the porch. "Hey," Jackson greeted, his expression clearly fraught with worry. "How did it go? Are you okay?"

Thomas saw the rounding of Chase's cheeks even from an angle behind him. Chase smiled and stepped up onto the porch and into his arms. "I'm fine," he assured Jackson. "Thanks to Alex."

Alex rubbed a hand over his face and shrugged casually, deflecting the praise he deserved. Thomas wasn't even sure he'd have thought of what to say and how to say it. "You did incredibly well." He glanced at Jackson. "I doubt they're coming back. The terms are... well, Chase can tell you."

Jackson led Chase inside with a nod, already focused on his lover again. "What are the conditions? Did he seem like he was gone?"

Cam and Noah stepped aside to let them past, then watched Thomas and Alex.

Thomas's cheeks burned as he felt the attention. He climbed onto the first step up to the porch, then turned around to face Alex. Alex stayed where he was just in front of the stairs, scuffing a foot on the ground. "Thank you for the help and the warning."

"No problem." Alex turned away to head to his car again.

Be bold. Thomas stepped down and grabbed Alex's arm to stop him. His heart raced. "I... actually, do you want to stay for supper?"

Alex's surprise was very evident. He stared at Thomas for

a moment, then stepped closer so Thomas could drop his hand from his arm. "If you'd like me to."

"I'm inviting you in." Thomas's heart was in his throat with nervous anticipation. He was speaking about more than just the meal.

Alex could tell; his eyes flicked rapidly between Thomas's as he examined his face. Finally, Alex relaxed into a smile. "I'd love to." He reached out slowly, tentatively, to take Thomas's hand.

Thomas couldn't help it; he looked behind him to the doorway first.

Noah and Cam were gone, leaving them to their moment of privacy.

Alex's expression flickered as he noticed the moment of distraction and he dropped his hand with a little smile. He strode up to the porch and past Thomas on the stairs to head inside as Thomas followed.

One step at a time, Thomas thought. At least Alex seemed to accept his hesitance easily enough. He just hoped Alex was patient enough to stick around until he had everything sorted out.

And, god, he hoped his brothers could get along with Alex now.

CHAPTER

Twenty~Five

ALEX

As Jackson and Chase sat close together at the dining room table, their voices low, the others gave them a minute or two of privacy. Noah fetched the condiments while Thomas set the table with placemats and utensils.

"Anyone want drinks?" Cam asked.

He memorized the orders as everyone spoke up with their choice of drink – beer, pop, or water. Alex went along with Thomas and asked for water. It seemed like a safe bet. "I'll give you a hand," Alex offered once everyone had spoken up.

"Thanks."

As Cam filled up glasses with pop or water and fetched two beers, Alex leaned on the counter next to him. "I wanted to say sorry to you one-on-one," Alex told him lowly.

"No, you don't have to."

Alex was surprised at how simple and sincere Cam's answer was. It wasn't passive-aggressive like he might have expected. "Wh-What?"

"You were doing your job. I get that, man," Cam laughed.

"I might have been annoyed, but you didn't break any laws. You got out of my face when I told you to. You didn't personally knock me out. My boyfriend's a little more annoyed, but he'll get past it."

Alex relaxed and smiled back. "Okay, cool. Just for what it's worth, I'm not taking that kind of job anymore."

"Oh, really?" Cam pushed a couple water glasses over to him. "Why not?"

"Um..." He stalled for a moment. "Just, it doesn't feel right. I was talking to Thomas and Chase in the car about it. Too much potential for me to make a bad call and hurt people. I got into this to help them."

Cam nodded. "You made the right call, whatever you said to them. I'm in a way better place now. Still miss the sport like hell, but..."

"Yeah," Alex sympathized. "I heard you got fixed up though. Any chance...?"

"Maybe." Cam's eyes were bright and uncertain. "I... um, I *could*. It depends on how the next few months go. They gotta test me again. If I ever collapse again, though, it's an ICD. And most teams won't want that kind of liability."

"Right, right." Alex fidgeted with his arm hairs, his chin on his fist.

Cam poured a pop for himself and Noah, then grabbed beers for Jackson and Chase. "The million dollar question... how do you know Thomas?"

Alex smiled sheepishly. *He told Chase now, so... I'm assuming it's fine...* "We dated in high school."

Cam's brows raised. He seemed stunned for a moment, but he recovered and nodded. "Right. Well, I hope you two work things out."

"What do you mean?"

"It's clear there's some issues right now," Cam chuckled quietly. "The way the two of you look at each other, though... There's chemistry. It's amazing. I've never seen it in him before."

Alex couldn't remember the last time he'd blushed. His cheeks felt hot, and he knew his face was turning red. He grabbed the two waters and a pop, balancing the three glasses in his hands. "R-Right. "Thanks."

Is he really that quiet about his dating life around his brothers? Why? To him, that was the million-dollar question, but it was one Thomas had to figure out himself.

Alex carried the glasses to the table, ignoring Thomas's curious look at his doubtless red face. To kill a few moments, he busied himself looking around at Jackson's gorgeous living room. Custom carpentry, metal art, and well-chosen paint colors made the house an oasis – far nicer than it even looked outside.

Then, Noah was pulling him aside as he brushed past him. "Hey, can we have a word later?"

Alex's stomach jolted with nerves and he nodded. "Of course." *He probably wants his chance to chew me out.*

Jackson clapped his hands together. He was now in the kitchen, pulling plates out of the oven as Chase carried them to the table. "Let's eat."

"When does the Fiddleheads' training camp start?"

From what Alex gathered, the new team was the same one that had tried to recruit Cam. They seemed like a pretty big deal, but not part of the major leagues.

He didn't know a hell of a lot about the minor leagues –

only the major teams. There were two especially hot teams in the Atlantic Provinces – Montreal versus Toronto. Everyone supported one or the other.

"April. I haven't heard who their coach is, though," Cam shook his head. "I was talking to Matty the other day about it. They have to announce it soon."

"How's Matty doing?" Jackson asked, his voice careful. About what, Alex had no idea.

"Pretty good. He's not getting a lot of ice time yet, but they seem happy with him so far. And he's loving the money," Cam laughed.

"I bet," Thomas nodded. "They ever gonna come out and see you?"

"The whole team? They'd have to commandeer the bus," Cam grinned. "But maybe Matty and a couple of the others. Or I might go see them when I have my next follow-up appointment, if they're playing near home."

"I wonder if Kevin will be signed," Noah frowned. "Does it work that way?"

"It could. It'd be a smart move. He's worth attracting if they can convince him," Cam nodded. "I'm still not a fan of the owners after what they pulled with me..."

Everyone was trying not to look at Alex. He quietly ate his last grilled green bean and listened.

"Yeah, but if the coach is decent..." Jackson shrugged. "Would you ever consider it?"

Cam leaned back in his chair for a few moments. "No. I'm... I'm done now. Now that I've been out for so long, even though the reason was shitty, I've... done so much more than I did there. I might have done more, but there's hundreds of other guys out there dreaming of getting bigger. None of us are gonna be the new 99."

Alex half-smiled. *Jesus, sounds like the wisdom of an older guy but he's my age.* "I think... there's that kind of pressure to be, and it could be pretty crushing sooner or later for most guys there."

Jackson glanced over at him and nodded. "Yeah, it can't be healthy."

"Yeah," Cam agreed. "You're exactly right. I can be way more effective here doing odd jobs and beekeeping and maybe picking up new skills than chasing a dream of making millions."

Thomas looked sympathetic. "You've been doing incredible work on all of our houses. Sneaking off sometimes to do it, but..."

Cam laughed and glanced at Alex. "I wasn't supposed to do any physical labor until this week, but I snuck a bit in here and there."

Alex grinned and nodded. That sounded exactly in character.

"It's a miracle he never killed himself," Noah muttered, fidgeting with his used utensils.

"Oh, come on," Cam grinned, slinging his arm around Noah's shoulders. "I'd have gone crazy lying in bed for weeks. And it was only a minor surgery."

"I think most people would disagree," Jackson laughed, pushing back his chair to gather dishes. "Anyway, we're all glad that's done now. Alex, you want another drink? A beer?"

Alex smiled, his eyes flickering to Noah pointedly. "No, thanks. Just stepping out for some fresh air, do you mind?"

"The back porch is shoveled," Noah told him. "I'll keep you company."

There was a moment's awkward silence where Cam eyed

Noah as if wondering if he was going to yell at Alex. Alex wasn't really sure about that himself.

Nonetheless, they let the two of them head to the back porch.

"That wasn't obvious at all," Noah snorted when the door slid closed and they shuffled close to the house. He pulled up a pair of dry lawn chairs and dropped into one.

"No," Alex agreed, grinning. "Just tell them you were yelling at me. That's what you're doing, right?"

Noah looked uncomfortable. "Not exactly. Actually..." He was swallowing his pride, so Alex gave him a moment of quiet to compose himself. "I want a word of advice." His lisp was even gone, his speech careful and proper.

Alex sat up straighter, knowing what this meant. "Professionally?"

Noah nodded. "If you... don't mind."

"Nope," Alex shrugged. "Go for it." He had a surprising number of people ask him everything from legal to medical questions. Being an investigator seemed to make people think he was an expert on every topic. He often had to turn away questions, but there were some he could help with.

"I found Cam's name on some gossip sites and... I don't know if I can get them taken down."

Alex winced and turned to face Noah, pressing his hands between his knees to keep them warm. "What sites?"

"Gay rumor sites. Cam has this asshole ex..."

"I know." Alex had found that out in his extensive research on the man.

Noah looked shocked for a few moments, then cleared his throat and nodded. "Right. Nathan?"

"Yeah."

"He sold their story to some online site. Crappy little gay

news site or something. I know he doesn't search for himself because he's worried about what people think about his... medical stuff... but."

Alex hissed through his teeth and leaned back. "So he doesn't know yet?"

"Yeah."

"You gotta tell him," Alex told him bluntly. "If you want my straight-up advice, that is. Someone he knows might Google him, you know? How bad is it? Is it true?"

"I... don't know how much is." Noah shook his head. "Asshole. I always knew he wasn't quite done. He... *apparently* he's notorious for trying to get back together with him. And Jackson got Cam to block his number, so he wouldn't have been able to get in touch if he were trying. Then he probably got pissed..."

"And sold the story," Alex finished. "Yep. Very plausible. Short answer, there's probably nothing you can do. The longer legal answer is that he might have some kind of libel case, but it's rarely worth taking it to court. You deal with really nasty stuff then. I've been in a lot of court rooms, and..." Alex trailed off. He couldn't really communicate the realities without sounding like he was fear mongering. "Believe me, it's absolutely shitty even when you're in the right."

Noah looked deflated.

Alex softened his voice to get Noah to look at him. "Listen. A lot of people, even minor celebrities, have this happen. Rumors on message boards, anonymous tweets, the whole nine yards. Nine times out of ten, when you react, you make it worse. Just talk to him about whatever concerns you – you know, if there's anything in there you're worried about it. And let it go. Do the others know?"

Noah shook his head.

Alex's heart warmed. Noah had at least a *little* belief in him, in order to confide in him. Or he was desperate. Maybe both. "Okay. Well, tell Cam first and let him decide if he tells the others, okay? Let me know if you need legal advice and I can put you in touch with people."

Noah looked grateful, then clicked his tongue. "Jesus," he murmured.

"Cons of dating an ex-celebrity," Alex winked. "But hey, if he has fans, they're not gonna be fazed. Every hockey player's got some kind of gay rumor."

Noah chuckled quietly, then rose to his feet. The night was too cold to stay out gossiping for long. "Okay. Thanks for your help."

Alex reached out to offer his hand to shake, searching Noah's eyes. He hoped this was an offer of friendship. Noah took it and shook. His grip was loose, but he smiled.

"I gotta get going soon," Alex told him and Noah glanced inside, then nodded.

They rejoined the others and there was another moment of silence, so Alex cleared his throat. "Thanks for having me over, guys. I better get going."

There was a moment of silence where Chase and Cam both glanced at Thomas while Noah and Jackson pointedly didn't.

Oh, man. I gotta talk to him about this tonight.

"Can I see you out?" Thomas asked.

"Of course." Alex's heart raced as he stood up and joined Thomas, ready to head out the front door. Thomas shoved his shoes and jacket on, then waved to his brothers. "See you guys later."

"See you," Cam waved.

"Thanks for visiting," Jackson told Alex, pausing to catch his eyes. "And staying for supper. Come over again sometime, if you want."

Alex didn't miss that invitation. He glowed a little as he smiled back. "I will," he promised. "Thanks for having me. Supper was great."

Chase paused to catch Alex, too. He leaned in for a quick hug and murmured, "Thanks."

"Of course," Alex answered sincerely. "Call me anytime."

Then, Thomas opened the door for Alex and led him through the crisp night to his own house right next door.

CHAPTER
Twenty-Six

THOMAS

"Want anything to drink?"

"You and your brothers are just plying me with drinks, aren't you?" Alex grinned, flopping onto the living room couch.

Thomas laughed. "Sorry, it's automatic." His nerves were fluttering as he joined Alex, sitting close to him and finally reaching out to touch his hand. "How was supper?"

"It was great." Alex seemed to mean that. "They really... accepted me. I definitely didn't expect that."

"They're a good bunch. None of them hold grudges – well, no, maybe Noah a bit, though he doesn't look it," Thomas corrected himself. "Was he okay?"

"Yep," Alex assured him with a slight smile. Then, Alex took his hand and caught his eyes. "Do you?"

That was a hard question, and it cut straight to the heart of what they had to talk about. Thomas drew a breath and let it out, then shook his head. "I have before, yeah, but... not anymore."

"You're okay with me now?"

Thomas almost shivered with nerves. His toe tapped on the floor. "Yeah. I... My family forgives you, and they had way more right to be pissed at you than I did. And back then, you needed different things than me. Dumping me made sense."

"I chose a shitty way of doing it, though."

"Yeah," Thomas chuckled quietly. "But we were both young. If you dump me again, though, tell me to my face and don't move away right afterward, huh?"

Alex chuckled quietly, but his gaze was fixed on Thomas's. "Deal. But I don't think that'll be a problem."

Oh. Thomas blushed under Alex's scrutiny but screwed up his courage. "I... I gotta talk to my family about this, though. I told Chase about us..."

"None of them knew?"

"No."

Alex nodded slowly, his gaze flickering between Thomas's eyes. "That's a big conversation. Are you ready for it?"

"Fuck, no," Thomas laughed quietly, his heart clenching. It wasn't like he was in *danger*, but... Christ, it was too hard to explain. He just shook his head. "But I know you need to date someone who's out."

Alex nodded. "My parents know about me. They'll want to meet my boyfriend. I want to be able to go out in public holding my boyfriend's hand." His fingers slid between Thomas's and he squeezed his hand lightly. "I better understand staying closeted now, but I still personally... can't maintain that. I... I told you I slept with guys for work, didn't I? I was actually a honey trap back in Ontario."

"Huh?"

"A guy who seduces men to see if they're cheaters."

Thomas's eyes widened. "Oh." After a moment of

thinking about it, he was okay with it, but his feelings were also complicated. "You don't do that anymore?"

"God, no," Alex laughed quietly. "It also sort of... jaded me. I can't do under-the-table relationships again."

Thomas understood instantly. Seeing Cam and Noah glow with joy when they did something as mundane as shoveling snow together, watching Chase tidy up after Jackson in the workshop... Every little experience he'd shied away from now seemed that much more appealing.

Damn it, he deserved that, too. And so did Alex. They deserved that... together. Thomas's heart soared.

Thomas's nerves crackled as Alex's fingers slowly rubbed against his palm. Alex massaged as he went, stroking the side of his thumb.

"So, is this just a booty call?" Alex murmured, his voice barely audible as he watched Thomas without looking away. "Or is it becoming more? I know what I'm feeling."

Thomas swallowed hard. "It's more, but... can we talk about this later? I need to talk to my family first. There's a lot of things I... never told them."

Instantly sympathetic, Alex nodded. "I understand. For what it's worth, I'm willing to wait a little while until you sort that out."

Thomas's lips parted with surprise and no small measure of delight at how easily Alex said it. Christ, maybe it *had* been him blocking Alex's attempts at rekindling romance all along. Not just *maybe*. It almost certainly was.

"I know," Alex laughed quietly. "You remember me as the last person who's likely to date or wait around for you. But I *do* want to do better, because you deserve better. And you bring out better in me."

Thomas nodded slowly. "Okay. All right, that's..." He was

glowing, a smile bursting across his face. "That's really neat. Nice. Cool."

He was almost stuttering with how pleased he was.

Alex chuckled, then raised Thomas's hand to his lips for a quick, sensual kiss of his palm, his eyes still on Thomas's.

Thomas licked his lips and grabbed Alex's hand. "Come upstairs."

For the second time that night, Alex accepted his invitation with a smile. He let Thomas pull him to his feet and guide him upstairs to the bedroom, his eyes on Thomas the whole time.

Thomas pushed the door shut behind them, then turned to Alex and took both his hands. He sidled closer to Alex and leaned in to press a long, slow kiss against Alex's lips.

Alex's lashes fluttered shut over those ridiculously gorgeous eyes and he parted his lips to let Thomas caress them with his own.

Thomas moaned and pressed into Alex, letting go of his hands to grab his hip with one hand. His other ran up Alex's sturdy back to the back of his neck, playing with the short hairs there. Alex was pushing forward, his lips surging against Thomas's as he gripped Thomas's hips hard and ground against him.

Oh, fuck, that set off a fire under Thomas's skin that couldn't be quenched. He growled under his breath and shoved Alex toward the bed. Alex paused to laugh, then grabbed him by the waist and pulled him onto the bed.

They were going faster this time, need clearly burning through them both. Alex hungrily undressed Thomas with his eyes and then his hands while Thomas slapped his hands away whenever he needed to yank Alex's clothes off.

"You're so forceful," Alex teased. "I like a man who knows what he wants."

They were naked, bare skin against skin, so Thomas relaxed and grinned up at Alex. "Makes it easier on you."

"It sure does." Alex knelt back over Thomas's thighs and knees, gazing up and down Thomas's body. Then, he reached out to run one finger down Thomas's chest toward his groin.

Thomas's cock was already hard. He sucked in a breath at the ripples of sensation under his skin from one simple but meaningful touch. When Alex reached the hair at the base of his cock, he circled around to tickle his inner thigh instead.

"Fuck," Thomas muttered, curling his toes into the bed. "Little fucker."

Alex laughed richly. "Oh, are you complaining?" He lifted his finger from bare skin and Thomas arched involuntarily off the bed, half-desperate for *any touch* to his red-hot skin.

"No," Thomas moaned, grabbing Alex's wrist to pull his hand back down to his cock.

Alex laughed and wrapped his hand dutifully around Thomas's cock. The way he handled him was so familiar and so... well, gentle, but not in a displeasing way. Thomas liked the grip firm, so that was what Alex was doing.

"That's it," Thomas whispered, his eyes drifting closed as he enjoyed the brief ring of tightness around his shaft. It slid down to the base and he moaned his approval. "You remember."

"I remember everything about you. All the things that made you gasp..." Alex twisted his hand around the top of Thomas's cock.

Thomas wasn't even trying to be funny – he gasped, right on cue. His head spun as the nerves under his throbbing cock flared with pleasure. "Y-Yeah..."

"And everything that made you squirm..." Alex pushed his hand down, twisting again to rub with his thumb. He hit the spot near the tip of his cock where skin pulled tight. It was a little button of pleasure, and Thomas resisted the urge to writhe for more.

"Christ, I didn't say come to bed to torture me," Thomas moaned.

"You're enjoying it, though. Little pre-come there," Alex teased. "But you do get wet pretty quick..."

"Filthy mouth," Thomas murmured, his cheeks burning. "Always liked that. Come on. Kiss me with that mouth. Put it to good use."

"I remember that, too." Alex crouched over Thomas and braced himself with his other arm, still slowly stroking Thomas's cock while kissing him like a porn star.

Better, even.

His lips were hot and wet and sensual, his tongue teased at the tip of Thomas's. When he sucked on Thomas's lip, Thomas's groan echoed against Alex's lips. Thomas's lips were already tingling and sensitive, but Alex wouldn't stop kissing them while stroking his hand slowly up and down the gradually slicker shaft.

"Y-You can't just... jerk me off," Thomas moaned his protest after a minute. His cock was fully hard and throbbing now in the air above his stomach, and Alex wasn't stopping stroking. He was kind of worried he'd wind up coming before Alex even got to town.

Alex breathed against his lips, "What do you want instead?" He was smirking, pulling back from the kiss slightly.

Thomas moaned his protest at being made to ask for it. He rolled his head back and Alex's lips instantly fell to his throat. Those lips – that distracting, skilled tongue – even the gentlest graze of teeth against his skin... All the while, the slow, firm grip slid up and down his shaft. Alex was bringing him along, not too fast, not too slow.

Thomas had never been with a guy who could give him this kind of sensual handjob and not make him want to kick him in the face. Thomas was *almost* willing to let Alex go the whole way with it, but also... no.

"F-Fuck, you're a cocky bastard," Thomas moaned and Alex's chuckle vibrated against the side of his neck where he was currently kissing and sucking. His lips still tingled as he gasped for breath, his stomach tightening briefly with a shudder of pleasure at an extra-firm jerking motion of Alex's hand.

He was sinking into bliss already and they'd barely started.

"Make love to me," Thomas whispered, his heart pounding. "D-Doesn't have to be rough... but more than... before."

"Either way," Alex murmured, his lips on Thomas's collarbone now, "it's not just a fuck."

Thomas jerked his head in a quick nod of agreement, then moaned and thrust into the tight ring of those rough fingers. "And stop tryin' to make me come already, Jesus."

Alex laughed and finally let go. "You don't think I can get you to come multiple times tonight?"

Of course, Thomas's body hated that sudden lack of sensation. Thomas moaned quietly as he tried to bring his body back down from the disappointment. "Filthy mouth," he muttered again. He loved it, though. Alex was utterly not shy about dirty talk in bed, and it was beyond hot. Plus, he seemed to like Thomas's direct language. Some guys got really weird about it.

He kept his eyes closed as he tried hard to catch his breath, one arm above his head and the other hand on Alex's back. "Y-Yes," he moaned when Alex's lubricated fingers touched between his legs. He pushed his feet a little further up and apart against the bed.

"You may feel some slight discomfort," Alex teased. "Would you prefer me to talk like that?"

"Oh, fuck off." Thomas's cheeks heated up all over again at the first penetration. Solid, wet fingers slid into him, simulating that first burst of pleasure from a man's cock pushing up inside him all the way to the base...

And Alex's cock made him feel *so* full.

"Or would you rather I whisper dirty nothings?" Alex breathed into his ear, pressing his lips to Thomas's lobe and the rim of his ear. "About how tight you are, how much your eyes glaze over with *gorgeous* pleasure when I fuck you, even with my fingers? How much I can't wait to be inside you again?"

"If you like," Thomas's voice cracked near the end of the last word and he cleared his throat, then gasped again as Alex rubbed his prostate.

Little shudders and flashes of pleasure built into steady sparks, then a dull roar. His libido was back in action, even if his cock didn't have any external stimulation at this moment.

Christ, maybe he could come just from Alex's skilled hips tonight. He couldn't *wait* to find out.

"But I don't just want my fingers in you." Alex's hand was sliding away, his fingers out.

God, now Thomas felt empty inside and he swallowed most of his answering groan.

"I know," Alex whispered in response.

Thomas heard rustling from the side of the bed, then

crackling closer to his ear. He cracked his eyes open. Alex was kneeling over him on all fours still, one arm braced next to Thomas's head, as he rolled the condom down one-handed. His thumb and forefinger pinched the tip long enough to keep it in place while his other fingers manipulated it down until he could safely bring his thumb down to help out...

And the cock slowly sheathed by that length? Alex had always been a shower, not a grower, and Thomas *loved* that about him. He could be shallow about one or two things, couldn't he? He chose to think so.

"Like the view?" Alex teased.

Thomas's cheeks burned and he nodded. "Love it," he admitted quietly. "It'll be even better when you get to it."

"Oh, sorry. Am I taking too long?" Alex grinned. "Do you even edge, bro?"

Thomas burst out laughing. "Fuck off and fuck me, you big..."

All he could think of were fond words. *Sex god. Protector. Patient, determined, smart.* Alex was everything he'd been missing for years, and now even more.

"I... I want you."

Alex grinned and Thomas's eyes flickered open to see if he understood that it was more than just sex. Alex's eyes were fond enough that Thomas suspected maybe he did.

"Relax, baby. I'm here," Alex whispered, kissing Thomas's shoulder. He lined up his cock with Thomas's slick, waiting opening and pushed inside.

That one kiss seemed more affectionate than any kiss to the lips. Emotion swelled in Thomas's chest and he nodded sharply, grabbing the back of Alex's head to kiss him.

Alex's breathing was shallow and quick, his eyes distant

as he pushed inside an inch at a time, until he was fully seated inside Thomas and his balls brushed the curve of Thomas's ass. Alex's arms hooked under Thomas's legs, pushing them up and a little further apart to bend him as he found just the right position.

"Yes," Thomas whispered, wishing he could hook his legs over Alex's shoulders. Maybe with skiing, he'd be flexible and strong enough for it. *That* was motivation to exercise, at least.

Alex kissed him affectionately, then sensually, and last of all, with the passion that surged through Thomas's own body. By unspoken agreement, Alex set into a deep, slow rhythm.

It was exactly like being jerked off a few minutes ago, only so much better to have Alex *in* him, their bodies locked together in passion.

"Alex," Thomas groaned his encouragement, grabbing Alex's shoulder blades first. He ran his nails slowly down Alex's back, enjoying every ripple of muscles he felt from Alex's slow, full-body thrusts. Alex's whole body undulated with the effort he put into it.

Best of all, Alex kept glancing in his eyes and watching his face for every ounce of enjoyment. He was an attentive lover, and Thomas loved that about him too.

"God, you feel great," Alex whispered. "This is perfect."

Thomas nodded before Alex even finished speaking. "So perfect..."

Every time he pushed down to the very limit, Alex filled him up completely, then pulled back and left him feeling empty for a second before he filled him up again.

The head of his cock rubbed over Thomas's prostate with each slow, firm thrust. It made little twitches of pleasure shudder through his cock and then his stomach and chest, all the way to his fingers and toes.

God, he burned with need for Alex, but the slow pace was everything he wanted. They had plenty of time later for fast, hard fucking to try and break the bed frame. Right now... they were sharing another moment, just as intimate as last time.

Alex gently kissed Thomas while pushing inside and Thomas arched against him, wrapping his arms firmly around Alex's back. Alex's cheeks were flushed, his eyes hazy with the same pleasure he'd whispered about into Thomas's ear.

Thomas carded his fingers through his hair once more before kissing Alex's cheek and nose and forehead, then back to his lips.

Alex laughed gently, his eyes lit up with wonder. "You're so playful."

"I hope you don't mind."

"I – nnh... not at all," Alex moaned, thrusting a little harder as he shifted his angle a little. "I've laughed more with you than ever, and I... like that."

Thomas nodded hard. It wasn't just sexual satisfaction – there was deeper pleasure here that he'd missed, and a much deeper connection than he'd ever felt to Alex before. This was an itch nobody else scratched.

He swallowed hard, then groaned at the sharper thrusts. "Yes...! You can go harder..." he whispered and was rewarded with several more kisses.

Thomas kissed blindly, his head spinning with pleasure as Alex gradually sped up his pace, still going hard and deep. Those muscled legs and arms held Alex perfectly steady even when Thomas grabbed at him.

"I'm gonna – any time now," Thomas warned. Another whimper was wrung from his lips as Alex thrust even harder, angled just right to rub inside him...

His cock was burning with desire to be touched. On the other hand, he felt so sensitive to every little brush against Alex's stomach or his own that he was positive he'd come on the spot if he were. Or maybe kick Alex.

Thomas didn't even have time to dwell on it. He gasped and shivered, his whole body tensing for a second with preparation as he felt himself hit that mental plateau right before the final climb and plunge...

"Come for me, baby," Alex whispered, kissing along his jaw and neck. "I missed you so much."

"I m-missed you too," Thomas moaned, his skin prickling with pleasant heat as Alex's chest rubbed against his and their hard nipples rubbed. Every little touch of bare skin, every brush of heat on heat seemed to multiply into a raging need for *Alex*...

Thomas clenched hard and rolled his head back into the pillow with another hard gasp as his muscles clenched.

"That's it, baby..."

"A-Alex... yes! *Yes!*" Thomas groaned. Even if he'd wanted to be shy and not vocal, there was no way he'd hold back the thoughts that whirled around his head. All were thoughts of Alex and how damn *right* this felt.

This was heaven, and he never wanted it to end.

As his body clenched and his passion squirted from deep within, he hit the moment of total focus. Every shiver of his muscles and slide of Alex's body against his only heightened the incredible sensation. Alex deliberately shifted his body to rub his stomach against Thomas's, trapping Thomas's cock between them.

"Yes..." Thomas whispered again, his voice hoarse. Bare skin and light hairs against the sensitive flesh made him *burn* all over again. He clenched extra-hard, his arms tightening around Alex for the last few pulses of pleasure.

Then Alex was driving hard and erratically into him, his breath coming in unmistakable, gasping pants. "T-Thomas... You're fucking gorgeous. Yes...!"

Thomas grabbed Alex's ass and pulled him in as close as he could to somehow get him deeper inside as Alex thrust and shuddered and gasped. Alex's face was incredible – he was staring at Thomas, not even through him, as if Thomas were the most beautiful sight.

Thomas flushed with embarrassment and pleasure, his breathing still hard and heavy as Alex gave a final few thrusts, then eased out and stripped the condom off.

Alex rolled onto his side and pulled him in to hold him silently while Thomas buried his nose in Alex's neck. Thomas twitched now and then with pleasure, his chest and stomach warm all throughout. His head still faintly buzzed. *That was incredible.*

"Christ, you're something," Thomas whispered.

"Thanks." A rumble of a laugh sounded in Alex's chest, vibrating against Thomas. "That *was* goddamn perfect."

Thomas scooted a little closer to push his thigh between Alex's legs and curl his arm under his head. "Only thing that's better..."

"Mm?" Alex pulled back enough to look him in the eye. It was easy to tell he was trying to remain calmly neutral.

Thomas grinned. "Wanna stay over tonight?" He *really* hoped his new-and-past lover would say yes. He'd hinted at it before, after all. "I work early tomorrow, though."

"Of course," Alex agreed instantly. "I do too. It'll be just like old times... only sexier."

Thomas laughed quietly and rubbed Alex's chest. "If you're lucky," he teased.

"I already got lucky."

The sincerity of the words made Thomas's smile falter for a moment before it came back with ten times the force. This was referencing more than their amazing sex. Alex was looking at him like he meant every damn word, not like it was one of his charming little acts.

"Shut up," Thomas mumbled, rubbing his face and sitting up.

Alex laughed hard with surprise. "You're not usually speechless. Did your inbuilt dictionary module get wiped during all that awesome sex?"

Thomas snorted and shoved Alex's chest. "You're getting an ego, and *I'm* getting up to wash off before I ruin my sheets."

"Heaven forbid you get a little come on them, 'cause nobody ever does that." Alex grinned mercilessly, hauling himself up in one easy sit-up to peck Thomas's lips.

"You..." Thomas smacked Alex's shoulder again as he stood up, but they were both laughing. He let himself into the en suite and cleaned himself off a little, taking a moment to gaze in the mirror.

This was who he was now. It was easy to see the change. Even to his own eye, Thomas glowed like he'd never seen himself glow before.

He *did* want to date Alex again – even that simple realization set his heart racing. He had to face everyone else first, but... Alex was willing to wait for him this time.

Thomas knew just what Alex had meant a minute ago. He was lucky, too.

CHAPTER
Twenty~Seven

ALEX

As the front door clicked shut behind him in the winter pre-dawn hours, Alex kept his steps quiet. He wasn't ashamed about leaving Thomas's house the next day, but he didn't want to attract unnecessary attention. Thomas still had to have conversations with both his brothers that might not be easier if they saw him.

Not that everyone wouldn't already know. He ruefully smiled as he unlocked his car and started it up. He shivered as he pulled on his gloves and grabbed the scraper. Luckily it hadn't even snowed, and there was just a thin layer of frost to scrape off the windshield that morning.

Alex worked quickly, laughing under his breath at the thought: if he'd wanted to make a quick getaway, lord knows he wouldn't be able to, what with Canadian weather conditions. Maybe he ought to invest in a car that would allow him to lock the doors while leaving it running in case he needed that someday after an all-night surveillance stakeout.

He climbed back in and pulled away from the curb, not

spotting many other cars on the road as he drove to his place first to grab a quick shower, change of clothes, and breakfast.

He had to get started early on his next case. He'd gotten the call yesterday just before the call about Chase's father coming into town: someone's cat was missing. It would have found a warm spot to burrow for at least the first couple nights, but he only had a few nights if he wanted to be successful. They were willing to pay his ridiculous rate for the full day of searching, especially around dawn and dusk.

God, it was hard to get up early some mornings, though. While he was alone, it was way harder, though, oddly. It should have been the other way – reluctance to leave his lover versus boredom in bed alone. Instead, being alone just... didn't treat him well.

The doctor had given him a waiting list spot for therapy, and he'd have to wait at least a couple months for that. In the meantime, he intended to keep himself focused, like always, on work.

Alex had a few ideas for this case, but he'd start in the usual places. Missing pet cases were among the best to solve, or the worst, if they went cold. Especially in the winter.

His first move was to search the owner's property, looking everywhere from gaps in the shed eaves to thoroughly searching the darkness under the porch. With no results, he broadened his search, looking around and over fences to see which properties he wanted to search.

There was a time he might have just climbed over and done it without asking, but he had to do things by the book now wherever he could. And besides, one of them might have some wisdom.

Look at me asking for help like a grownup. Alex wryly smiled as he knocked on the first neighbor's door.

Every neighbor let him search the yard as soon as he explained what was going on, and they told him they hadn't seen any cats but would keep an eye out now. One offered to put out a box and blanket, while another offered to help search after work that night.

Then, a few houses down, one of the neighbors said something interesting.

"I think I saw an orange cat darting around a snow bank yesterday afternoon, actually. It was near the garbage shelter."

Ohhh. Alex's eyes widened. He hadn't even considered the shelters – large wooden boxes some people put near the end of their driveway to house their bins. Most were sealed pretty well, but if one wasn't, it would provide a neat little hiding place...

"Thanks," Alex nodded hard. "I'll follow up on that."

It took him a little while to search the nearby shelters. He didn't turn anything up, nor had he seen any paw prints, though there wasn't any newly fallen snow.

Every now and then he stepped back into his car and warmed it up, to give himself a little break from the cold as morning crept into late morning, then afternoon. He finally had to take a break to eat the sandwich he'd brought and drink some tea, though his eyes still wandered around the street as he sat in the car and watched.

He might only have one chance to spot the creature. Unlike most of his cases, this was literally life and death.

It was around two when Alex got another lead from neighbors two streets away. They said that yesterday, they'd seen something orange going around the snow to the shed behind them, but that place was empty most of the time.

They'd thought it was a trick of the sunlight since it had been sunset.

Good enough for him. Alex thanked them, and then waited until they were inside the house again before doing one more search of their yard.

When he was sure nobody was looking, he hopped over the fence to the other place. The snow hadn't been touched here since winter began, and had formed into a hard ice pack. Certainly no paw prints around, but the wooden shed was what he was most interested in anyway.

Alex stepped back to have a good look at it. The doors were jammed shut by so much snow around them, but there was a mound of snow that had blown up next to one side of the shed. When he had a closer look, he spotted a gap in the eaves.

"Aha," he whispered. He took another glance at the house, then rubbed his chin. He couldn't go about this wrong... the cat could escape one way while he searched another.

Then, Alex had a crazy little idea that made him grin.

Stepping back, he stomped on the ground until his boot broke through hard ice and snow. He bent down and scooped up the boulder-like chunk of ice and snow, then shoved it up into the gap in the eaves. Once he searched the rest of the perimeter, he found two more easy gaps and shoved snow chunks in them, too.

Now for the hard part. He had to stomp a few more times – enough that he was considering going back to his car for a shovel – before he managed to break through enough snow to kick it away from the doors.

Alex bent down and clawed with his gloves, grateful they were waterproof, to pull pieces of ice and snow away from the door. The shed was unlocked, though there was a clear spot where a padlock could be threaded to keep it locked up. He was exceptionally grateful for that – getting a cat out of a locked shed would be damn near impossible.

When he yanked on the doors, they didn't budge at first. He had to bend down and scrape at the snow again, muttering to himself about weapons laws. They weren't allowed to carry anything, just in case. That ruled out the Swiss Army knife that would have been damn handy right about now.

Still, with enough scraping that his fingers nearly went raw, even inside his gloves, he managed to get the corner free and pulled open the door again, staying low to block the cat's escape in case it tried to run for it.

Like magic, it was there and it wasn't even running or fighting.

It just meowed loudly and trotted up to him.

"Aha, I bet you smell the good stuff, huh?" Tuna salad sandwich for lunch. "I saved a bit for you..." He knelt back and pulled off a glove, ignoring the sting against his fingers, to pull out a bag of cat treats.

The cat – Joker – was already climbing on his knees. He laughed as he tried to keep its face out of the whole bag of treats. "I see why they call you Joker. Your mom's worried sick about you, you know." He fed it a couple of treats, then tucked the bag in an outside pocket and reached out to carefully scoop him up.

Just as he'd been told, Joker didn't offer any resistance. He awkwardly pulled his glove back on, the cat in his arms, then rose to his feet.

Thank god the police weren't waiting for him when he hopped back through the neighbor's yard and side yard to the street. He doubted they'd give him trouble when they learned what this was about, but it was still technically tres-passing.

"Not that I care, huh?" he asked Joker, shifting him in his arms as Joker purred harder. "Hold on, gotta get you in the back seat..."

He might as well not have bothered; as soon as he climbed into the driver's seat, Joker climbed into the passenger seat and tried to nose at him for more treats.

"Oh, you're hungry, aren't you? I'm bringing you right home, buddy," he promised. "Just sit tight. Don't get under-foot. Shoulda picked up your cage first..." Kaylee had told him he wouldn't need it, and he'd believed that.

Joker sat on the driver's seat, digging in his claws as Alex pulled away. Alex kept nervously glancing over, worried that Joker would try to interfere with his driving, but Joker was more patient than he'd expected.

When he pulled up in front of the cat's house, Alex crawled backward out of the car and reached across to tempt Joker closer with a treat, then scooped him up again. He didn't bother locking his car, just keeping Joker tight against his chest as he walked carefully across the slippery street.

The door was already open by the time he was there, and his client was hugging first Joker, then him. Alex stood back with a smile, watching Joker press his head against her face before running for the food dish.

"Well, he's learned better, I hope," Alex laughed.

"Thank you so much. Do you have your invoice now or should I pay later? I'll pay on the spot," Kaylee offered.

"Don't worry about it. I'll email you tomorrow," Alex told her with a smile. Her face flooded with joy again as she hugged him. "Just – enjoy being with him again."

"I will," Kaylee said with a sincere little smile. "If anyone else ever needs your help..."

"Feel free to pass my name along," Alex agreed. "I can't always help, but I can do my best. Your Joker was a pretty easy one to find, at least." He'd only bill her for seven hours, since he'd taken a few minutes off to warm himself here and there.

Alex still glowed as he drove home, marveling that it was only three in the afternoon.

His glow only faded a little when he reached his apartment and found it empty and quiet. Compared to the Rileys' houses, there weren't people around all the time. Nobody was there to greet him, and there wasn't someone friendly right next-door.

Alex smiled slightly again as he thought about supper last night. That had gone pretty damn well, all things considered.

Nobody was obligated to be around him. He had to get his own life in order. The more he did that, the more Thomas seemed drawn to him, which was a bonus.

Maybe it was time to focus his work on things he really liked: catching cheaters, finding lost pets, and just helping people. No more revenge or corporate cases.

Alex knew he made enough money doing what made him happy. He wasn't supporting an extravagant lifestyle anymore, and the cost of living here was way better. And now that he'd been working here for nearly a year, people were referring him to their friends, meaning more of the same kinds of cases he wanted. He could finally unclench his fears a little. Unlike Thomas, he didn't have bosses to navigate or please.

And Thomas... if he wanted to, Thomas would eventually come to him. His phone went off seconds later, giving him a shock. They must have been on the same wavelength for a moment.

Hi, I had an amazing time. Do you want to come for drinks with my bros + friends tomorrow night? Then we could go to late supper and date... xx

Alex answered fast, eager to see more of that wonderful smile.

Me too. I'd love to see them and especially you again. What time and where?

Thomas texted him the name of a bar downtown that Alex recognized well and told him to come at 6 p.m., dressed for a nice supper.

Ooh. Sounds intriguing ;)

No sleuthing! It's a surprise.

Alex laughed. The surprise was just which restaurant Thomas would choose, but nonetheless, it was a nice one.

Okay, he agreed. Then, he added, *Can't wait. What are you doing today?*

Just got off work, going out to talk with my bros soon.

Alex felt nervous on Thomas's behalf. Was this the big talk? He wasn't sure how to respond except to wish him well.

Good luck! Have fun xx. He scrolled through the emoticons for a minute before finding the right heart icon – the simple red one – and adding it to the end of the text. Then, he hit send.

A minute later, he had his answer: the same heart emoticon in return.

Alex smiled and pocketed his phone, trying to turn his attention to cleaning his apartment so he could burn all his nervous energy off on something useful and avoid crashing on the couch to do nothing for the next day.

Though last night felt like moments ago, tomorrow night

felt like it was an eternity away. No doubt Thomas's conversations tonight would determine how tomorrow night went, and maybe many future nights.

Be brave, he thought to Thomas, half-wondering if he should have texted it. *You have nothing to lose... and we have everything to gain.*

Twenty~Eight

THOMAS

"So, Thomas, what's your answer?"

Thomas's heart thudded as he gazed across the conference table to Barry. The man's tie had a few threads out of place and it was driving him nuts. *Not the point.* He raised his eyes to Barry's now and straightened his shoulder.

This was perhaps the hardest decision he'd ever made. He'd have given anything not to give this answer.

"No, thank you."

Barry looked stunned. "You... don't want it?"

"Not at this time. I don't think it's appropriate, given... recent events."

Barry waved a hand. "I don't know what you mean." He winked and Thomas's stomach twisted; he'd been right to turn it down. "This is just the most qualified man getting the job. Are you sure about that answer?" he pressed.

"I just can't do it yet, sir. I look forward to getting another offer in the future if my work merits it," Thomas told him. "And I'd like Irma to know that this is still my goal, but not yet."

Barry looked deflated as he nodded. "Right. Well... thank you for getting back to me." He rose to his feet and shook hands again.

Thomas walked tall as he left the office.

"What happened?" Georgie whispered, leaning in. Sam, Chris, and Kyle were all busy serving customers, but she sat next to him and there was nobody else in line right now.

"Not much. He wanted to know what I thought about a few things," Thomas lied. "Compared to Halifax."

Georgie looked disappointed. "Oh. We all thought you were getting a job offer."

Thomas's stomach lurched. *I can't tell them... can I? Would they be jealous? They might wonder why...* "Why?"

"You're obviously the best-qualified. You're young, but you've got the degree. You're really good."

Thomas's cheeks felt hot and he cleared his throat. "O-Oh. I see. Thanks. I try..."

"Take the damn compliment," she laughed and rolled back to her window, waving the next customer to enter the bank over to her window.

Thomas blushed and closed his mouth, then glanced over toward the offices. Barry was approaching Irma now, and the two of them stepped into Irma's office.

It was only a couple minutes before Barry emerged again, his coat on and briefcase in his hands.

Oh, my god. She threw him out. Thomas bit back his grin and nodded slightly, but he didn't look over as he passed on his way out the front door.

Irma wandered after him, leaning in the doorway of her office.

When Thomas looked over at her again, Irma offered him a slow smile and nod.

Thomas's anxiety faded instantly.

*That **was** the right thing.*

It was only later that afternoon, not long after lunch, that he brushed by her in the hall and she reached out to stop him for a moment.

"I hear you weren't ready for more responsibility this week," Irma told him with a meaningful smile. "Would next week work?"

Thomas hesitated. "As long as it's not..."

"*This* meeting's with me, not that oily bastard."

Thomas's jaw dropped. He hadn't heard that kind of language in the bank before from anyone, let alone Irma. "I..."

"Oh, don't look so shocked. We all think that about him. So, yes or no?"

"Yes," Thomas murmured, smiling back. "Thank you."

"Good job today, kid." She nodded briskly and kept on walking.

Thomas glanced after her, then slowly walked on to the break room. Irma's respect was worth ten times more to him than any offer Barry could have made. If he was going to get an offer from Irma, he knew it was because he was the right man for the job.

Or if she just wanted to praise Thomas for turning down the offer from the "oily bastard" today, he was fine with that too. He couldn't help it; by the time he got to the break room, he was laughing about it. Maybe he should be a little more like Irma.

Before Thomas even pulled away from the curb after work, he sent a mass text to both of his brothers.

Hey guys, you two wanna come out to the bar with me tonight? Save our guys' night for tomorrow night instead?

He got his responses within moments from Cam and only a minute later from Jackson. Both were enthusiastic yeses.

That left him with one person to text.

Alex's fond responses made him smile broadly as Thomas suggested a date, which was quickly accepted. He wanted to see Alex around his family and friends more. He couldn't keep these parts of his life separate, and he didn't want to.

Best of all, though, were the heart emoticons Alex sent at the end of the conversation.

Thomas's cheeks burned with pleasure as he stared at it, then sent back the same heart to Alex. He pocketed his phone and tried to calm down, but he ended up pulling it out again to have one more quick glance at it before he drove.

Alex was hinting at the same emotion that bubbled in Thomas's chest whenever he spent time around Alex... or even thought about it. Even all these years later, their feelings had never truly faded. It felt completely natural for them to be flickering back to life, but much stronger than before.

And now, Thomas was strong enough to admit it to everyone else: he was a sucker for this gorgeous detective and his better ways.

"You're kidding me."

Cam stared at the laptop screen without really seeing it yet, still processing Noah's words. Noah had his arm around his shoulders, and he'd just told him a few words he'd never expected to hear.

Nathan was back.

Well, not really. This article was dated a couple weeks ago, but he hadn't even thought about Nathan in fuckin' *forever*.

"How dare he?" Cam whispered, finally focusing on the headline. It was sensationalistic, just as he'd expected. Some gossip blog or news site, some crap, talking about closeted gay sports stars; the piece featured Nathan's account of their relationship.

Cam scanned it and shook his head. Some of the details were right: they'd had a tumultuous off-and-on relationship, yeah. Others were *wildly* off base: the off-agains hadn't been caused by his own internalized homophobia and fear of discovery.

Christ, Nathan had spun this to make himself look like a little angel. That was probably what ground Cam's nerves more than anything.

"I can't believe he'd do this."

"Or that he found someone to pay him, presumably."

"Is it paid?"

Noah shrugged. "It could be for revenge. He sounded like an asshole."

Cam pushed his laptop back and pulled Noah closer. "Yeah, he was. All that... it's half-true, but..."

"It's fine," Noah murmured. "I believe you. You don't have to explain yourself to me."

Cam still burned with the urge to explain: *I* wasn't dumping him; *he* refused to meet my family; *yes*, we fucked in a locker room once, but there was nobody else in the damn building, and it wasn't the fuckin' main Toronto arena!

He let out his breath and nodded, then looked at Noah. "How did you find out?" Then, something clicked. "You were talking to Alex..."

"I asked him what we can do," Noah murmured quietly, fidgeting with the hair at the back of Cam's head. "He told me it's pretty much nothing. Unless we sue people for libel or whatever, but he said... well, he didn't think court was fun."

"Right," Cam murmured, his thoughts still absent. Had any of his teammates heard about this? Matty would have told him, right?

He pulled out his phone and sent Matty a quick text.

Some shitty article out online about me. Don't look it up please. But it's mostly garbage.

Matty was still his closest friend from the minor leagues

out in Toronto, though he'd been drafted to play with the big boys now.

Then, Cam looked at his boyfriend and blew out a quiet breath. "Anyway, I'm not getting back into it. Nobody I care about will think twice about the story. They all knew about us."

Noah silently nodded.

"And..." Cam trailed off thoughtfully. Matty had texted back.

No problem man. At practice now. TTYS. We gotta Skype.

Cam quickly answered,

Yep we will soon. See you buddy.

"Good, Matty's cool with it. He'll deal with everyone else if they nose around," Cam told his lover. "And Alex helped? You two are on good terms now?" He'd kind of thought Noah would be pissed off.

"I hope you don't mind--"

Cam kissed Noah to silence him, then smiled gently. "Of course I don't. If Thomas is gonna date him..."

"We don't know that," Noah reminded him.

Cam laughed. "You heard the car starting up this morning as well as I did."

"Now who's a gossipy little bastard?" Noah told him off, but he was grinning, too.

"I'm just saying," Cam winked. "And now he wants to come out to the bar tonight to talk to Jackson and me."

Noah just smiled quietly, then closed the laptop lid and turned on the TV instead.

God, Cam hoped this was the beginning of Thomas opening up. It was about time, for all of their sakes. And if he was finally seeking love, about *fucking* time for his own sake.

Please, let Alex be trustworthy.

CHAPTER

Thirty

ALEX

"How's work going?"

The question that had stressed Alex out since last year no longer held as much weight, even coming from his parents.

He could honestly answer, "Great."

"Any interesting cases?"

"Yeah. Today I did a missing cat. Found it by three o'clock. He spent last night outside, though... it's a damn good thing he found a great shelter."

"Oh, poor thing," his father frowned, setting down his knife and fork. "Good for you. Do you think business is picking up?"

"Definitely. This client found me through another client, who found me through another... I'm at three referrals deep, and I think that's the critical mass. From everything I learned in the business class at college, anyway."

Probably more useful than the classes on surveillance or the law had been the business class where private investigation students learned how to run their own businesses. Most did, though a fair number joined the bigger security services companies, too. Given his employment history, Alex hadn't exactly had a choice.

"So you think you're going strong, even not doing insurance cases anymore? They aren't the end of the world," his mother told him. Before she could gather up their dishes, Alex stood up to do it. "Oh, thank you."

"No problem." Alex stacked plates. "Yeah, it's going fine. But I'd really rather not, for now. For as long as I can get away with it. I have more inroads in personal cases now. Insurance and business cases can be steady if you do the same thing for the same firm over and over, but that's... not why I got into it."

His parents exchanged looks.

"Honestly," Alex insisted, setting the plates in the sink and returning to their dining room table. "I'm fine. I have work and friends to keep me busy. And something else I wanted to tell you." His heart raced; this was an early announcement, so he wanted to keep it casual. He also wanted to spread the news.

"Oh?"

"There's a guy I've met. I'm sort of seeing him, we're still figuring things out, but we're interested in seriously dating."

"Oh, congratulations. Who is he? Do we know his family?" his father asked.

Alex laughed. "Dad, stop it. You'll meet him soon if he's not too shy. He's still coming to terms with everything."

"Don't get your heart broken by someone who isn't proud enough to be with you," was his mother's advice. She spoke with a frown of concern.

Alex reached over to squeeze her hand. "I won't, Mom, I promise." Ironic, though. That was just about what had happened last time... though he'd done the actual dumping, it had been after Thomas told him he wasn't coming out.

It was six of one, half a dozen of the other for their past faults. He trusted Thomas again now, and vice versa... perhaps even more strongly now that they'd hurt each other before. Broken and fixed trust ought to be weaker, he thought, but it was just the opposite.

"Good. We hope we can meet him sometime," his father followed up. "When he's ready."

"Thanks," Alex smiled. He laughed when his phone went off in his pocket, then checked the caller. *Oh, it's not him. That would have been weird, twice in a row.* He didn't know the number. "Sorry, I should take this for work."

He stepped onto the porch and shut the door, shivering as he stayed close to the house. "Hello, Alex speaking."

"H-Hi. I'm calling about your services. I actually, uh, heard about you. My buddy Chase was talking about what happened the other day. My name's Floyd."

Floyd... I know that name. Oh! "You own the tattoo shop he works at."

"Oh, you know me. Yes."

Can't exactly tell him how if Chase hasn't told him I tracked him down... "Yes, I do. Go on."

"I have a sort of problem. I don't know if you can help, but... in case you can."

"Of course. Do you want to speak over the phone or in person?" It was a bit of a trick question since Floyd sounded nervous and he'd already guessed he didn't want to talk over the phone.

"In person would be great," Floyd told him, sounding relieved.

"Is it urgent?" Alex wanted to spend the evening with his

family since he'd be out tomorrow – and as many nights soon in the future as possible – with the Rileys. "Should we meet tonight?"

"No, tomorrow or whenever you're free is fine. Evening works better."

"How about the day after tomorrow? Are you working that night?"

"I can close the shop and we can talk there, yeah. Good idea," Floyd answered. "I'll see you then. Oh, one more thing..."

"Yeah?"

"Can you not tell the Rileys about this yet? They're my friends and all, but... especially Chase."

"Of course. As soon as I consult with a client, confidentiality applies," Alex told him. "That's no problem."

Floyd sounded relieved. "Okay. Thanks, man. See you soon."

"Bye," Alex told him and hung up, then tapped his phone on his lips. *Very interesting.* It could be something as simple as a background check on an employee – though he doubted it, with how nervous he sounded – or it could be more.

He'd find out soon enough.

CHAPTER
Thirty-One
THOMAS

THOMAS'S HANDS ALMOST SHOOK AS HE CARRIED BACK A couple beers from the bar to the table. "One for you, one for you, one for me."

He slid into the booth by his brothers, trying not to feel dwarfed by them. His whole life had been that way, really. They were just big and broad guys, whereas he was built like a twig. He was okay with it personally – it just made them look kinda funny when they were all out together.

"Thanks," Cam answered while Jackson nodded. Cam cradled the beer, not sipping it yet. He had to make it stretch longer, after all.

"So, I wanted to talk to you guys about... relationships and stuff. You probably guessed," Thomas laughed faintly. His stomach was twisting with anxiety, making it hard to stomach the beer.

The brothers exchanged looks and nodded. "Yeah, we did," Jackson confirmed.

"I told Chase, so I may as well tell you: I dated Alex in high school."

For a moment, none of them said a word. Thomas was holding his breath, waiting for the reaction – good or bad.

Then, Cam slapped the table and made both Jackson and Thomas jump. "*Fuck*, yes! I knew it."

Jackson punched Cam lightly. "Jesus, take a year off my life, why don't you?"

Cam laughed and shrugged, still looking triumphant. "Sorry, but I knew it. I've been waiting forever to hear that."

"You suspected?" Thomas asked.

Cam shook his head. "No real proof, if that's what you mean. You hid friggin' *everything* from us, man."

Thomas felt a little sheepish.

"Yeah, he's right. Why didn't you say?" Jackson watched Thomas closely, his expression soft and more concerned.

Thomas drew a breath and let it out, then sipped his beer to give himself a moment. He had a speech rehearsed, but it was gone now. "I... thought it was weird for us all to wind up gay."

Jackson raised his eyebrow. "Why?"

"Pretty cool, though," Cam smirked. "Triple the cool factor. Three gay families in one neighborhood! That Christian school will have to reroute their school buses..."

"Cam," Jackson laughed. "We're having a moment." Nevertheless, Thomas laughed and shook his head, too.

Cam raised his hands in apology. "Sorry."

Thomas turned back to Jackson to explain. "Um, like I was copying my big brothers or something."

"You aren't copying being gay. Do you like being in bed with him?" Cam asked.

Jackson laughed but looked at Thomas.

Thomas's cheeks heated up and he nodded. "Yeah."

"And you like being romantic and shit?"

Thomas nodded again.

"Then you're one-hundred-percent full homo milk, baby."

Jackson snorted. "I'd have put it a little gentler, man. I mean, he could still be bi."

"Oh, oops."

Thomas laughed, his tension already fading as he watched his big brothers banter. "No, it's okay. I'm not. I don't think. I don't... really feel into a lot of people, actually. But Alex was always something else."

"So back in high school..."

Thomas winced. "Yeah, that was another thing. You guys stood up for me because I wasn't gay. But really, I was..."

"No," Jackson told him firmly. "We stood up for you because you didn't deserve to be picked on, not because you were being called gay when you weren't. I don't give a crap about the bullies' factual accuracy. I gave a crap about people not being picked on for stupid shit. Or any shit, really. You little idiot," he added.

Thomas was blushing now. He rubbed a hand back through his hair and laughed, almost too flustered to say anything. "I... I don't know. I built it up into this huge thing."

"Sometimes those huge things are just completely things you invent in your head," Cam shrugged. "They still feel big. But I'm glad you came to us."

Thomas still had a nagging little fear or two, though. "But Alex, specifically?"

"What about him?"

"Don't you guys kind of resent him still? Isn't it weird for me to date *him*, of all people?"

"I never knew you cared what others thought," Jackson

half-smiled, but his teasing was gentle. He was right; Thomas usually either didn't care or did a damn good job pretending he didn't.

"But no, we don't," Cam chimed in. "We talked about it afterward. He was doing his job both times. We were just worried that – you talked to Jackson about some kind of work thing, and we were worried he was somehow screwing you over."

"Who, Alex? No, no," Thomas hurried to explain.

"He wasn't investigating you or something to do with you?"

Thomas shook his head firmly. "Definitely not. He was just keeping an eye on me for a while, until I was ready to... talk to him again, I guess. We never really got over each other." It was bizarre to be admitting his feelings to his brothers, even over a beer. He couldn't quite look either of them in the eye.

"Why's that? I mean, he's your ex. Did you break up on good terms?" Cam asked. This time, Jackson looked worried.

Thomas hesitated and shook his head. "But we were a lot younger then. We talked through it all."

"Still," Jackson added. "Be careful if you decide to date your ex again."

"Of course." Thomas smiled to himself, gazing at the head settling in his beer glass. "I think I was just waiting for him to grow up, and... for me to, too. I know you don't like exes dating..."

"Just 'cause we've had bad luck doesn't mean you will," Cam said firmly, looking over at Jackson like he was soliciting agreement.

Jackson hesitantly nodded.

"Nathan was shit for a long time. I knew that *before* we

broke up. The last time, I mean. You know we broke up more than once – Jesus, it must have been four, five times. It was really off-again-on-again," Cam told them. "And last month, he sold our story to some online paper. It's only a really minor piece. You have to search for my name to find it."

Thomas straightened up; he'd never heard this much. "Oh. What...?"

"Yeah. It's all bullshit, so I'm ignoring it. And anyway, we "mutually" broke up most of those times, but..." Cam trailed off, shaking his head. "He moved in and out. He tried to control which of my teammates I hung out with. Luckily I never cared what he wanted me to do, but if I hadn't been so pigheaded..."

Thomas shivered. "I didn't know that. I just thought he was a dick, all... weird and cold toward you. Jackson told me a little. And I didn't know it was *that* off-and-on. Fuck."

"You gossiped about my boyfriend?" Cam grinned at Jackson.

"When you're dating a dick, that happens."

"Fair enough," Cam laughed. "And there was you and... Ed?"

"Oh, Christ, don't even talk about Ed," Jackson groaned.

Thomas laughed. He remembered the man who'd moved in with Jackson just as well. They'd given a relationship two shots, the second of which was even worse than the first. They just hadn't clicked together, and after the honeymoon period of living together for a week, it had been fights all the time. He didn't like seeing Jackson like that. He was so much calmer now that Chase was around.

"But like I said, this could be different," Cam said, looking back at Thomas.

Thomas couldn't express how grateful he was for the benefit of the doubt. He hurried to confirm, "It is."

"Okay," Jackson smiled, raising his beer. "Here's to that."

They clinked glasses and sipped, Thomas's eyes flickering at last between his brothers' faces. They both seemed genuinely pleased, not pissed off at him. He felt even more stupid for waiting so many years to talk to them.

"So is it looking like you'll date again?"

After this conversation... hell, yes. "Yeah," Thomas nodded. "I'd already decided I'm gonna date him again. I just wanted to tell you first."

"Oh," Cam laughed. "Suppose you'd better let him know next."

Jackson joined in his laughter. "Sounds about right. There's our stubborn Thomas back."

Thomas grinned broadly. "Yeah. Don't worry, I'm not roping him into anything." Far from it – he was stepping back into Alex's waiting arms.

He was one of the few people stubborn enough to resist Alex's charms, deal with his bratty moments, and better yet, let Alex lead when he had to. But he was done resisting.

"I invited him to come along for supper tomorrow. I figure all our boyfriends and friends will be there. Especially if I tell them what it's for," Thomas grinned. "That'll be a surprise for him."

Jackson choked on his drink. "Oh, Jesus, you're wicked."

"Yeah," Thomas agreed, grinning and sipping his beer again as he leaned back in his chair. "Just quietly so."

"Damn right," Cam laughed. "Try to be a little less quiet next time, eh?"

That was their way of asking Thomas to trust them with

his secrets. He trusted them with more than that – with his life. He just casually nodded and raised his glass.

"Yep."

That was all he had to say in order for his brothers to understand.

Thirty-Two

THOMAS

THOMAS PATTED HIS HANDS TOGETHER, THEN STOOD UP straight as he spotted the peacoat-clad figure of his boy-- his *lover*, he reminded himself sternly.

"Hey," Alex called out with a little wave, walking carefully around an icy patch. When he finally reached Thomas, he shook his head. "Jesus, the city must have run out of its salt budget for the year."

Thomas laughed, taking Alex's hand once he was close enough. His cheeks burned, but he stretched up onto tiptoe to give him a hello kiss.

It was quiet and gentle, and full of affection.

"Oh... *hello*," Alex murmured, pulling back after a couple of seconds. "You all right?"

"Never been better," Thomas grinned. "You got all dressed up. I see you chose your pinstriped shirt."

"Yes, sir."

"You always liked pinstripes on your test days. You said it was a lucky charm."

"Oh, man." Alex laughed. "I forgot that. And you look adorable."

Thomas laughed, glowing with appreciation. He'd chosen a chunky gray knitted scarf and a different shade of gray V-neck sweater over a collared shirt.

It seemed like an appropriate outfit to come out in.

"Are your friends and brothers here yet?"

"Yeah, you're the last one."

Alex groaned. "Oh, I hate being the last one."

"Really? You don't like being the center of attention?" Thomas teased. He knew Alex had his moments where he did.

Alex hesitated, then shook his head. "Not when it comes to meeting important people."

"It's not a huge deal," Thomas assured him with a smile.

"They're important to you, so they're important to me. Speaking of which, what have you told them? I don't want you to feel uncomfortable..."

Thomas smiled softly at Alex and leaned in to peck his lips again. "There's rumors is all. I didn't want to assume anything when I told them, but... they know we're seeing each other."

"Okay," Alex grinned. "Cool. I'm glad." He looked much more excited than Thomas had expected.

Thomas smiled back, then led Alex into the bar.

It was noisy that evening and busy, but they'd managed to find their own table big enough to cram a bunch of their buddies in – Floyd, Ryan, Kevin, Ashley, Chase, Noah, Jackson, Cam, and now Thomas and Alex.

Alex actually went pale for a moment, and Thomas grinned. *Oh, my god.* He'd never actually seen Alex visibly nervous before, so the fact that he was now made Thomas's heart squeeze. He was telling the truth about wanting to make a good impression on them.

Thomas loved him all the more.

"Hey, guys. This is Alex."

"Hi." Alex waved, looking around at them. "I kinda know a couple of you... I'll try to remember your names." He slid into one of the two empty chairs they'd all left next to each other and Thomas took the other as they introduced themselves.

Thomas smiled, leaning back to watch.

"Want a beer? Jackson offered. "I'm about to get a round."

"Oh, thanks," Alex nodded. "That'd be great."

A waiter passed by and Jackson flagged him down, then asked for a round of beers.

"So, what do you do?" Ryan asked. "I heard something about being a cop..."

"Oh, no. A private investigator," Alex chuckled. "Kinda like a cop but we can't carry weapons."

"Is it dangerous?" Kevin asked.

Alex relaxed, like he'd had this conversation a hundred times. He probably had; Thomas had been just as fascinated when he found out what Alex wanted to become. "Oh, it can be, but it's not as dangerous as the movies make you think."

"Anything happen here?" Ashley asked.

Jackson grinned at Thomas and Thomas just rolled his eyes and laughed.

"What?" Ashley insisted. "I'm just askin'."

"Everyone wants to know about my most dangerous stakeout," Alex grinned. "It's okay. I just can't say much. Client confidentiality. Um, I *can* say that I once had to watch someone all day during a blizzard, building my own snow shelter in the woods to watch from the edge of their property... and then I found bear tracks in the fresh snow."

"Jesus," Thomas muttered. He hadn't heard that one, and all of a sudden he worried a little more for his lover's safety.

Alex grinned and shook his head. "That's rare, though. A lot more of it is just stuff like cheating spouses, lost pets, missing persons."

"Don't the cops deal with missing persons?"

Alex's expression faded into a grimace and he looked around. "Anyone friends with the cops here?"

"Oh, boy." Kevin clapped his hands. "We're getting to the juicy stuff and we haven't even gotten our beers yet."

This set off a round of laughter.

"We work together sometimes," Alex shook his head. "Some are great. Others around here are... well, you saw the headlines. Otherwise, Google them sometime if you want."

Thomas nodded. He read the newspaper, though most of their friends didn't. It was hard to find New Brunswick-specific news otherwise.

"They just can't do everything we can, and vice versa. Sometimes they have bigger things to worry about in a particular time or year. Sometimes people don't trust the cops, but they trust someone outside of them."

Ashley was nodding thoughtfully.

"That's pretty cool," Jackson agreed.

"How did you meet?" Kevin grinned broadly, and a few others – Thomas included – groaned.

"Nosy bastards. You don't have to answer," Thomas laughed. "But, for the record, we knew each other from school."

"No kidding. That's a long time."

Alex smoothly answered, "We dropped out of touch for a

while. Then when we both moved back here..." *He tracked down my brother and my other brother's lover and then bumped into me...*

They exchanged grins for a moment, both clearly thinking the same thing.

Jackson chuckled under his breath.

"Cool," Ryan said simply. "Oh, here's our beers. Cheers!"

They all clinked glasses as best they could, then settled back to drink. It only took minutes before they were involving Alex in conversations, asking about his hobbies and who he knew here.

Thomas relaxed while Jackson shot him a *told-you-so* look.

As bizarre as it was being open about who he was now, nobody had even commented. With two gay brothers already, he had the easiest time of all. Their friends could be assholes sometimes, but only in a friendly way and Alex could handle himself.

Maybe this was gonna work out okay.

CHAPTER
Thirty~Three

ALEX

"That was really fun."

That was the third time Alex had told Thomas this since arriving at the nice Italian place just a couple blocks away, but he meant it. In the eyes of all their friends and family, it looked like they were already together, and they'd accepted him.

And then Floyd had caught him in passing to murmur that he didn't need to meet up anymore. Everything was fine now, Floyd had said. It hadn't really been the time to quiz him so Alex had nodded and let it go. That aside, things seemed fine with everyone.

And then Thomas had taken his hand for the walk over. Alex had never thought Thomas would be at this stage. He'd never dared to hope as much.

They just had to say it. Saying it out loud made it formal, and Christ, it made them both vulnerable all over again.

But vulnerability also made them stronger, and Alex saw that now. There was something incredible about entrusting each other with their hearts for the second time, even knowing what had happened last time.

This time, they'd work things out.

"I've got another cheating husband case tomorrow," Alex murmured. "This one should be a lot easier to prove, if she's right."

"Don't you get tired of that?" Thomas asked. "I mean, it must be hard."

Alex bit his lip. "I... actually let it influence what I thought about relationships for a while," he admitted slowly. "And I was really depressed. I'm getting a little better, but it's worse in the winter. So that influences what I think."

Thomas sucked in a slow breath and nodded. "I see."

"I'm getting therapy."

"Oh?" Thomas looked startled. "I'm glad for you."

Alex smiled to himself. "Me, too. I'm... I'm trying," he promised. "I hope I can get a little less... rough around the edges. Maybe a little more hopeful. I talked to my parents not long ago, actually, on that note. It was kind of weird, but nice."

Thomas settled back as they waited for their main courses. "What did they say?"

"Um, that they had to work hard at things." Alex caught his eyes, scooting his chair closer to the table and reaching out a hand.

Thomas silently rested his fingertips so they lightly entwined with Alex's. He nodded again.

"Just that they were already similar enough that things worked out, but then all the minor differences, they had to work through... nothing we haven't heard before."

"Yeah. Jackson's really big on that, too."

"He's big on a lot of things."

Thomas laughed, making Alex smile too. "Yeah. He's a bit hotter-tempered."

"I remember that much from school."

"Oh, right. Of course you would."

It was easy to forget that they'd known each other so long. So many more important things had happened over the last couple of weeks.

Their sparkling cordial – non-alcoholic, Alex had insisted, since he had to drive – arrived. They let go of each other's hands.

"I'm ready for something steady," Alex admitted slowly, swirling his glass around like it was wine.

Thomas smiled and nodded. "Me, too. Actually, I wanted to talk to you later, but... no time like the present. You said you were willing to wait..."

"Mmhmm." Alex watched him, trying not to get his hopes up again.

"I've talked to everyone now. My family's cool. I'm cool. I just... I think I'm ready."

Alex raised his eyebrows, his lips slowly curving into a smile. "You want to be my boyfriend?"

Thomas let out a quiet breath and nodded, his eyes locked on Alex's. "I was just waiting for you to seriously ask."

"Over the summer, I asked," Alex hummed. "What changed?"

Thomas laughed. What *hadn't* changed? "Both of us."

Alex paused, then chuckled and conceded the point with a nod. "Good point. So, boyfriends?"

"To being boyfriends." Thomas picked up his glass to clink with Alex's, and then they sipped.

It wasn't an earth-shattering moment like he'd once expected. It was the quiet whisper of something that had long been out of place slipping into just the right spot in his life.

Alex wasn't leaving; Thomas was ready to admit it to himself and everyone.

"On one condition," Alex smirked after a moment of the words settling in the air.

"Hm?" Thomas narrowed his eyes suspiciously as he smiled.

"You let me teach you to properly ski."

"Oh, no," Thomas groaned theatrically. "I can't afford to break any more gear."

Alex laughed, settling back in his chair. "Are you afraid?"

Thomas looked hesitant. "Maybe a little."

"Fall off the horse ten times, get up eleven."

Thomas snorted, almost choking on his cordial. "I don't know how many horses you've fallen off, but you might have a concussion."

Alex had to cover his mouth before he burst out in impolitely loud laughter in the middle of the formal restaurant.

"If you insist, I suppose," Thomas winked.

Before the winter ended, Alex would drag him back onto the slopes again. Despite Thomas's theatrical reluctance, Alex could see him looking excited about the idea. After all, this time they could cuddle in front of the wood stove afterward.

"Valentine's Day is coming up," Alex winked, leaving the suggestion in the air to see how Thomas felt about it.

Thomas didn't even hesitate for a moment, just nodded firmly. "Perfect. It's a date."

Thirty-Four

THOMAS

"We could go to your place."

"No," Alex murmured, catching Thomas's eyes as they made their slow way along the freshly-salted sidewalk to his car. "I'd rather go to yours."

Thomas blinked. He preferred his own place, of course, but why did Alex?

His confusion must have shown on his face. "It... It feels more homey," Alex told him with a sheepish smile.

"Aw, you don't like your apartment?" Thomas frowned, swinging their hands lightly between them. "It's an okay little place, just plain."

"Exactly. Yours looks comfortable."

Thomas laughed. "I can get Noah to help you decorate," he teased. "He'll get your house sorted out. He did all of ours, and we're still tweaking and adding things. Jackson's always making metal art pieces now, too. He got really inspired last year."

Alex grinned. "Cool. But does that offer apply to my new house, if I wind up moving?"

"I thought that was a ruse!" Thomas stared at him. "You *are* getting a mortgage?"

"What, a ploy to investigate? No," Alex laughed. "Not completely, anyway. I've been thinking about moving. I don't want to live in an apartment for more than a couple years."

Thomas hummed quietly and squeezed Alex's hand. "How much do you value living alone right now?"

Alex slowly looked at him. "I'm... not a big fan of it. Why?"

"Well... I know we only just agreed to officially date, but looking forward... what do you think about living with me? Maybe a year or two down the road, maybe a few months?" Oddly, Thomas didn't feel as nervous as he'd expected.

"I'd like that," Alex answered. He didn't even take a moment to think about it, which told Thomas he'd been thinking about it himself. "I... I'm a little jealous of your brothers."

Thomas laughed quietly, leading Alex around a patch of ice before stepping over the snow bank toward his car. "Me, too, sometimes. They're so much further ahead... and always have been."

"Really? God, you've got so much lined up already," Alex told him firmly. Thomas's spirits lifted at the sincere encouragement. "You're a couple years younger than me, and god, I barely have my own shit sorted out."

Thomas laughed. "I think I was an adult from... pretty much high school on. I just always focused on the future."

"As long as we take time to enjoy the present." Alex let go of his hand and circled around to the driver's side while Thomas gazed thoughtfully at him. When Alex saw him watching him, he laughed. "Get in before you think about that."

Thomas obeyed and climbed into the passenger seat,

buckling up. He rubbed his hands together and stuck them between his thighs. "That's very wise."

"I meditated on the ski mountain to learn that."

"Really?" The moment he asked, Thomas groaned. "Shut up."

Alex snorted. "You almost believed me."

"Almost. Not quite." Thomas grinned anyway, pressing his hand against Alex's knee and rubbing lightly as Alex pulled away from the curb.

The air in the car warmed up as the engine ran, and by the time they were back at the group of three houses, it was *almost* toasty.

"That's the worst thing about winter," Thomas groaned. "You can park up in the driveway behind me."

Alex looked startled at the sudden complaint, then concerned. "What is?" He pulled up into the driveway.

Thomas smiled. "It's nothing," he quickly reassured him. "Just that the car gets hot right when you get where you're going."

"It's better than being in Toronto where you're stuck in traffic for so long your car gets hot and stuffy." Alex pulled the parking brake, shut off the car, and grinned at him. "Or Montreal, where they swear at you in French."

Thomas laughed, climbing out of the car. "I've never lived anywhere but here or Halifax, and I don't really want to. Everyone else seems to have and nobody likes it."

"That's not true." Alex stayed by his side as they walked up to the front door. "There's Vancouver, all the artsy guys and drama students smoke pot with cops... Alberta, where everyone gets rich and shares STDs, unless the price of oil keeps dropping..."

"Oh my god," Thomas laughed under his breath as he

unlocked his door. "You're not selling them to me."

"No?" Alex grinned. "I didn't mind Toronto, actually. Certain parts."

"Like where?"

"The gay village. C'mon, that's pretty cool. Have you visited?"

"Not really," Thomas smiled. "I went out to see Cam a couple times, but we never went there."

Alex feigned shock. "He didn't take you? How lax."

"He wouldn't have known I'd be interested," Thomas grinned. "Besides, you know I don't do clubs."

"There's more than just clubs. There's cafes and book-shops and nerdy places."

That didn't sound half-bad. Thomas nodded. "We can go out there sometime, then."

Alex hung up his coat and kicked off his boots. "Good. I'll take you someday." People would forget him by then. Give them a year or two and he'd get a warm welcome in most bars.

"Thank you for looking out for my cultural education," Thomas teased, hooking his thumbs through Alex's belt loops to pull him closer.

Alex winked. "Oh, of course. You're getting a late start. It's my duty."

"Why, 'cause you're the first guy I dated?"

Alex went still for a moment, his eyes widening.

Thomas turned red. Now that he thought about it, he'd never told Alex that. He'd hinted that he'd been more experienced than he actually had been back then. "Er, first *real* date. I mean, I kissed other boys before you..." *And god knows I slept with other men afterward.*

"I was your first-ish...?"

Thomas nodded, letting go of Alex's belt loops and sliding his hands to his hips. They felt perfectly right settled there, his thumbs on Alex's hipbones. He was a bit scrawny; Thomas would have to feed him well.

"And you still want me? Usually people run *screaming* from their first," Alex snorted.

"Not sleep with them years later?" Thomas laughed and sidled closer to press his lips against Alex's. *He's so worried about what I think, too. Did the depression come with a low self-image or something?* He murmured, "You weren't, and aren't, half-bad."

Alex relaxed, an embarrassed little smile crossing his lips. "C-Cool."

Thomas decided he'd spare Alex from more compliments just yet. Considering how egotistic he pretended to be, he really couldn't handle them. "I missed you," Thomas murmured. "Would it be rude if I pulled you right upstairs?"

The embarrassment faded into a pleased grin on Alex's face. "I don't think so. I might be biased, though."

"Excellent." Thomas winked. "Then come upstairs."

Alex slid his arm around Thomas's waist and squished him into his side to walk upstairs side by side. He rubbed Thomas's hip and thigh, then up his side. "I missed you, too. I went to talk to my parents last night."

"Mm?"

"They'll want to meet you sometime, if you're cool with it. And I wouldn't mind meeting yours. I vaguely remember them, but it was a long time ago."

Thomas smiled at the memory of sleepovers with Alex, or studying together. They'd usually gone to Alex's parents' house, but they'd spent a little time at home, too. Alex had just strategically avoided times when the other boys were home. Cam being at hockey all the time, that hadn't been hard.

God, they'd snuck around for so long.

"I wouldn't mind," Thomas admitted. "Your parents were nice. They were always relaxed."

"Wonder if they guessed."

Thomas shook his head. "You had a lot of friends. Unless you dated them all..." Alex had always been the stud with a bit of a bad boy vibe. Getting his attention at all had been miraculous, even if it had just been to help him with math homework at first.

Thank god it had turned into more.

Alex closed the door this time, then turned Thomas around gently and pressed him up against the back of it.

He had *no idea* how hot that made Thomas. Thomas trembled for a moment before bracing his legs firmly as Alex pressed his leg between them and ground their bodies together slowly. Their lips met as naturally as the horizon met the ocean – gently at first, then harder, with swells of emotion.

Lust wasn't overshadowing stronger sentiment, though. Thomas moaned and grabbed Alex's hips to force his body as close as possible. Trapped between the cool, solid surface of the door and the heat of Alex's body, his body tingled with pleasure.

"You *love* a little manhandling, don't you?" Alex murmured.

Thomas nodded hard. "And you know how to handle me," he whispered. "You can do a little more, though."

"What did you have in mind?"

"Surprise me."

Alex's fingers closed around Thomas's wrists, pulling his

hands above his head. "I can think of a few ideas... but give me one."

Thomas's cock hardened between them a little more, the blood rushing south as his eyes widened. Christ, he was into this, whatever it was.

"You can lift me, I bet. You're strong," Thomas teased.

He didn't have to drop any more hints: Alex let go of his wrists. His sexy lover grabbed his ass and hoisted him into the air.

"Jesus--" Thomas grabbed Alex's shoulders, trying to wrap his legs around his waist. "A *second* of warning!"

"You told me to surprise you."

"Dick," Thomas laughed as Alex crashed onto the bed with him. He squirmed under Alex, keeping a firm hold on him to roll him over. He was on top now, Alex under him.

"Oh," Alex murmured, his eyes widening. "Well, then."

Thomas unbuttoned Alex's shirt, kneeling back to admire him. It was a lot easier to get a great look at him from this angle instead of underneath.

God, he was strong. Those abs rippled up into a tight stomach and muscled chest with well-defined pecs. His biceps rippled as he shifted his arms to help Thomas pull the shirtsleeves off. The angles and planes of his body caught against the light, framed by wrinkles in the comforter underneath him. His hair, short though it was, was spiked up against the pillows.

Best of all, Alex's cheeks were pink, his eyes already bright and sparkling with anticipation.

"I'm not behind my brothers in one respect," Thomas told him. "I picked the sexiest boyfriend."

Alex laughed in surprise. "Well." He ran a hand down his own stomach. "You mean the gym time paid off?"

"Definitely," Thomas winked. He pressed his hand over Alex's cock, a stiff bulge in his dark jeans. "I want to lick those abs."

Alex groaned, and Thomas felt his cock twitch under his hand. He had to be going half-crazy for more attention.

Thomas winked and pulled his hand away after rubbing the bulge just a couple times. He shrugged his own shirt off, almost tangling his head in it before managing to get it free.

"Need a hand?" Alex smirked.

Thomas tossed his head. "I'm fine." He braced himself over Alex, kissing at the side of his neck and along his collarbone.

Alex took no time to respond to that, his chest rising and falling quickly. "Oooh. Now who's the tease?"

"Fair's fair." Thomas intended to take his time. He kissed along Alex's ear and behind it, then along his jaw and under his chin, down his throat...

With each press of warm lips to hot skin, Alex twitched or tensed or moaned very softly. It was incredibly fun, and he hadn't even gotten to the good part.

Thomas kissed slowly down his chest toward one nipple, smirking as Alex's moans went up a pitch when he was an inch or so away from the sensitive flesh. *There's all those nerves...*

"Thomas..." Alex whispered in a hoarse breath.

"Mmhmm?" Thomas kissed a slow circle around the nipple, never straying closer than an inch away. What delicious pecs he had, though. Christ, he was built.

Alex chuckled breathily and didn't say anything yet, but when Thomas glanced up, his eyes were dark with hunger.

Thomas took mercy and licked slowly up the curve of his chest, then over his nipple.

"Ah..." Alex's head fell back and he pressed his feet into the bed, his fingers curling hard into Thomas's shoulders.

Christ, he had a strong grip.

Thomas flicked his tongue across the stiff nipple a few times. Another groan, this one harsher, escaped Alex's throat and Thomas's lips curved in a wondrous smile. He wondered just how much of Alex's body was as sensitive as he remembered.

Thomas flicked his lips around a nipple, then sucked it into his mouth and ran his tongue around it again.

"Oh, your mouth's even better than I remember," Alex breathed out. His grip had relaxed slightly as he kneaded Thomas's shoulders.

Thomas licked all the way over to his other nipple and sucked harder, pinching the nub between his lips and flicking his tongue harder.

Alex arched off the bed. "Ah!"

Thomas soothed the spot with a few kisses and a wink, then scooted backward a little at a time, kissing the whole way down. He took particular time kissing each of those ridiculous abs. He mouthed at the sensitive skin, sucking until Alex was twitching and moaning.

Alex was nearly a mess, but he had one more thing to do first.

Thomas fumbled with his jeans to pull them open and down and Alex arched his hips gladly to help him get his clothes off. Thomas yanked his own jeans off with less care. When Alex was ready to take over, he wanted to be ready.

Alex's cock bobbed free, stiff and pink above his stomach. It was a point of pride that *he* was fully responsible for teasing it to this state, and he wanted to please Alex a little more.

Alex hardly seemed sure what to do with his hands – he kept touching Thomas's shoulders, upper arms, and hair lightly. He shifted a few times, trying to get a comfortable position. "I-I'm tested, I'm all good. If you were thinkin' about that."

He's... not used to letting someone else take over. Thomas shot a perceptive little glance up to Alex's face and smiled. "Okay. Me, too."

"For everything?"

Thomas nodded. "So, you know, when you get bored of this... if you want to forgo condoms..."

Alex's eyes widened at the implication. He almost sat up, but he shifted again, his thighs spreading a little more. "Cool. Yeah. I'd love to. I mean, we're boyfriends..."

"Just relax," Thomas whispered and kissed along his thigh toward his stomach. Then, he kissed the base of Alex's cock, lapping his balls for a few moments before working his way up the shaft.

"Nnnh." Alex seemed to be struggling to lie back, but he finally let out a deep breath and did so, his eyes half-closing.

"Mm," Thomas moaned his approval, then closed his lips around the head to suck gently on that sensitive part. It was salty, yet tasty; it had been years since he'd last tasted him, but he'd remember the taste of Alex anywhere. God, he loved it.

He bobbed his head slowly, taking the velvety, smooth shaft all the way down. He licked along the veins and the underside the most, keeping his lips carefully between his teeth and the smooth skin.

Then, once he was confident he had the right angle and he wouldn't hurt his lover, he drew his head up and bobbed back down. He set into a quick, wet sucking rhythm.

"Hah! Nnh, Thomas-- yeah," Alex whispered. Despite his relaxation, he was tensing now from arousal. His thighs clenched, his stomach tightened... When Thomas made eye contact, he was squeezing his eyes shut and rolling his head back as his chest heaved for breath.

Thomas paused now and then to lap at the head and the sensitive spot on the underside of that thick cock. He kept stroking the base of Alex's dick with his other hand, keeping it hot and tight for him.

"T-Thom-- you're-- Jesus, I'm gonna come in *minutes*."

Thomas almost snorted with laughter, but his mouth was too full. He just slowly pulled his head up and off the shaft, not even minding that his jaw faintly ached. That would go away in minutes. The expression on Alex's face – strung out from pleasure, slack-jawed, staring at him like a sex god? That would be imprinted on his memory forever.

"Then show me what you've got first," Thomas whispered, kissing his stomach and chest. He barely got one lick in before Alex grabbed him and hauled him the rest of the way up, rolling them over to pin Thomas down. "Yes...!"

Alex ground against him, his wet cock sliding against Thomas's only slightly moist but very much throbbing hard-on.

Thomas's eyes widened and he gasped. "Oh, Christ."

"You always liked a little dick-on-dick action," Alex whispered. His voice dripped with filthy suggestion. "Someday, I'm just gonna hold you down and make you come by grinding against you." For emphasis, Alex pulled his hands above his head, lacing them with his own fingers. Alex's hips moved in slow, skilled circles to rub the sensitive shafts together.

"Christ, I was in your backseat once," Thomas

complained, though his heart pounded with arousal at the words. "Don't need to do that again."

Alex laughed loudly and winked. "It's more fun now. See?" For emphasis, he ground hard, Thomas's cock burning at the friction between them. The firm, throbbing shaft against his gave him plenty of sensation that nothing else could compare to.

"Fine," Thomas whispered. "But not tonight. We need to celebrate."

"That we do." Alex let go of Thomas's hands and went for the lubricant without being directed to, helping himself to a generous squirt of it.

Thomas gasped at fingers pressing up in him but pushed his feet into the bed and gritted his teeth with pleasure. And then Alex was rubbing his prostate like the teasing little fucker he was.

Not that Thomas was much better. Thomas had loved teasing Alex with foreplay earlier, and he'd do even more of it next time.

"You're so gorgeous," Alex whispered. "I hope it doesn't get old that I say that so much."

Thomas chuckled. "I'll find a way to deal with it," he teased. "Mmph." The teasing fingers only made him crave something a lot bigger and harder. Within a minute, he squirmed and shook his head, his eyes closed as he struggled for breath. His body was sparking and tingling, throbs of pleasure running through him from head to toe. "I'm good. I'm *more* than ready."

"Yeah?" Alex murmured.

The fingers in him slid out, leaving him disappointingly empty. Thomas kept his eyes shut for a few moments to try to catch his breath while Alex finished getting ready.

The moment he felt a hot, hard cock head with a surprising texture rubbing against him, he remembered the offer he'd made. His eyes snapped open again with surprise.

"You all right?" Alex smiled, bracing himself but not pushing in yet. "I can do a condom if you'd rather. It's not a big deal."

"No," Thomas whispered. He wanted to be Alex's in a way that made him burn with embarrassed but wholehearted pleasure. The thought of being claimed from the inside out set his heart racing.

"Okay. You ready, baby?"

Thomas nodded and whispered, "Make love to me."

Alex didn't even look surprised, but his cheeks rounded into a beautiful smile. His white teeth flashed and his eyes glittered. The joy on his face was indescribable, and Thomas committed it to memory, too.

He hoped he remembered this day for years to come.

Then, the slow, hot slide inside him as fullness burst through him, followed by fiery pleasure. "Hnnh!" Thomas groaned, grabbing Alex's hips and digging his nails in to haul him in.

"Yeah," Alex moaned, his cock sliding in without resistance. He filled Thomas perfectly, though it was a tight fit. It was just perfect for them both. "You're..." Alex trailed off, shaking his head as he gazed at Thomas. Alex was fully seated now, his cock utterly filling him while Thomas squirmed underneath

Thomas couldn't even catch his breath as he shifted his feet around and rolled his head back. "Hnnh. Yeah...? I'm what?" he whimpered. "Oh, Jesus." He needed that cock surging in and out with the power of Alex's hips.

What the fuck was he waiting for? Oh, this was almost

perfect...!

"I love you." Alex's Adam's apple bobbed as he swallowed hard, his eyes locking with Thomas's. "I'm sorry if this is fast-
-"

Thomas let out his breath and whispered, "I love you too, of course, you idiot. I never stopped." He cleared his throat and grabbed Alex's face to haul him down for a quick, sloppy kiss. "Now get moving before I die of blue balls," Thomas moaned his exasperation.

The laugh against his lips from Alex's surprise sounded gorgeous echoing around the walls of his bedroom. Thomas grinned, then relaxed as his tension was finally satisfied.

Alex fucked him tenderly and slowly, his cock pushing in and pulling out at an incredible, deep, slow pace. He was so patient, and it made Thomas's heart flutter in ways even he would never admit.

"Yeah..." Thomas moaned, sucking Alex's lip between his own as their eyes shut. Their noses bumped and they panted against each other's lips now and then.

The cold of the car and the outside air was long forgotten now. Alex kept smiling, and Thomas even thought sometimes it might be unconscious. He didn't even seem to realize he was doing it.

Ecstasy wasn't far away as the bed creaked and Alex's gasps turned from soft to loud, voiceless to moaned. Thomas wasn't shy about groaning his pleasure and approval when Alex found just the right angle.

When Alex sped up, it was by mutual agreement. "Yes!" Thomas groaned, slapping Alex's ass lightly. He loved feeling those muscles clenching under his hands with the effort Alex put into it, even if he made it seem like nothing.

Alex kissed him until he lost all rational thought, and

then a little longer. Alex's hand pinning down both his wrists until Thomas's hands curled into fists with the desire to stroke his own cock was almost the last straw.

Alex's hot, tight hand around his cock, jerking him off at the same hard, twisting pace he so loved *was* the last straw.

Thomas spilled over the edge all at once, groaning and arching off the bed, clutching at Alex's shoulders and clenching hard around him. "Yes! Yes, Alex... don't stop..." He threw his head back as his passion spilled from deep within between their friction-hot bodies. "Alex!"

"Yes, baby," Alex moaned against his cheek and jaw, then bit his neck. "I'm-- yeah! Thomas, d'you want me--"

Thomas's eyes flew open to see that beautiful face clenching in ecstasy. "*Yes*," Thomas hissed, tightening his grip so Alex couldn't pull out of him.

Alex's cheeks flushed with pleasure and amazement, and then he came. His warm joy flooded them both, and Thomas's chest and cheeks burned at the utterly new feeling.

"Yes," Alex moaned, kissing near his ear as he tried to catch his breath and pound into Thomas a couple last times. "Oh, god..."

Thomas tightened his arms around Alex's back, hugging him close as both their bodies went still, save for their heaving chests.

He never, *ever* wanted to let this man go again.

Alex pulled out but not away, rubbing his hand over Thomas's forehead to brush his hair back and affectionately kiss him again.

Thomas moaned, then gave Alex a loopy little grin. "Perfect."

"Just what you ordered, hm?"

Thomas nodded, almost too exhausted to even answer.

As his breath returned, so did all other thought. Though he'd braced himself for bittersweet emotions, none came; there was no regret now in Thomas's heart.

"That was... incredible," Alex whispered. The way he watched Thomas told Thomas that he felt it, too. Something subtle was happening now – maybe some post-sex hormone making them feel closer. Whatever the case, he couldn't stop watching Alex, either.

Thomas murmured, "We can do that again. Lots of times."

Alex chuckled deeply, the sound reverberating through both of their bodies. "Especially when we don't see each other for a day. Jesus."

"I can't help what you do to me," Thomas grinned. Alex made him prickle with pleasure to look at, even when he'd already finished. Come to think of it, round two wasn't off the table.

"How about if we did this all the time? My lease is up in a couple months, and I... well..."

"Move in," Thomas whispered his invitation, his eyes widening hopefully. Christ, the only better thing he could imagine than dating and loving this man was getting to live with him, too.

Alex grinned. "I can't say no to that face. I'd love to."

Thomas kissed his lips until Alex laughed and rolled his head away for breath, then kissed his cheek a few more times. "Perfect. When's your lease up?"

"March."

"That's *two months* away," Thomas complained.

"I'll spend enough time over here," Alex chuckled again. "Besides, we have work to keep us busy. And we can plan which side of the bed we'll sleep on..."

"Dibs on this side," Thomas told him. "You better like the

other."

Alex snorted and turned his face away to laugh again, then pecked his lips. "I love you," he reiterated simply.

"Love you, too." Thomas rolled carefully onto his side, caressing Alex's cheek and hair. "Speaking of work... I never told you. I reported it, and some sleazy manager offered me a promotion. I'm assuming to stay quiet."

Alex nodded. "Did you take it?" he asked carefully.

"Fuck, no. I really wanted it – you know how much I wanted it... but no. Then my actual boss, the head honcho here in the branch, caught me in the hall and said she might be hiring next week. I think... she's gonna offer me the job again."

"Would you say yes this time?"

Thomas nodded. He'd had a little time to think about it, and the more he did, the more he liked the idea. "If it comes from her, it's not a bribe. It means she believes in me. And I can do so much good. I can help people out in weird situations. You know, single parents or gay couples or groups of friends... people lenders usually don't like."

Alex nodded thoughtfully. "Making good out of a bad situation."

Thomas hadn't thought of it that way, but he nodded. "I think so, yeah. I've always wanted to do this. To be more than on the front lines. It would be... more fulfilling."

"I'm sort of doing the same thing. I'm dropping a lot of companies and working on personal cases," Alex murmured. He carded his fingers through the light hair on Thomas's chest. "I can afford to now."

"As long as you don't have to become a honey trap again," Thomas murmured with a faint frown of concern. "I'm not judging what work you take."

Alex shook his head. "No, I know. It's not about that. It's honestly... something I need to do for me. I need more faith in people."

"And investigating cheating assholes will do that?" Thomas laughed.

Alex nodded thoughtfully. "Cause it's not them I'm doing it for, it's the loyal people on the other end of it who got hurt. I want to help them get the strength to walk away."

The words hung between them for a few moments. Thomas smiled slowly and touched Alex's cheek, then kissed him again. He wouldn't compliment him on being noble because Alex would just turn that compliment down, but he believed it.

Alex had a damn good heart, and Thomas was lucky he'd given it to him.

It had been a challenge, and he knew now that sometimes the biggest challenges didn't come from outside forces. The obstacles Thomas had built up were all in his head, but challenging them was a thousand times harder than standing up to peer pressure from some other person. He didn't give a crap about other people, but facing his own desires was the hardest thing he'd done.

Thank god Alex had stuck around for him. This time, Alex had understood what was wrong and how to help him. And Thomas could see it on Alex's face: Alex was happier now. Maybe not cured yet, not the best man he could be, but he was getting there.

This second time around, they were trusting each other with more than just their hearts. There was a whole life together to look forward to. Sure, it would be messy and complicated sometimes, but it was worth fighting for that future together.

FOUR MONTHS LATER...

"Here's to the first year!"

Bottles clinked all around in a cacophony of glass as the Riley brothers, their family, and their friends celebrated.

"And," Jackson continued, still standing at one of the picnic tables in their shared backyard, "to us. Me and Chase, Cam and Noah, and our newest couple..."

A chorus of "Awww"s, predictably enough, sounded from everyone as all eyes turned to Thomas and Alex.

Thomas turned beet-red and even Alex blushed under the scrutiny, but they held up their bottles in answer.

Since moving in a couple months back, the last vestiges of tensions between Alex and the other brothers and boyfriends had vanished. That night with Chase's family had done wonders to ease the tensions.

It helped that Alex was doing better these days – brighter and happier, getting out of bed easier. He attributed it to therapy, more sunshine, but most of all, Thomas.

Their love was clear in the way they watched each other.

"Now kiss!" Kevin shouted while Ryan groaned and Jackson laughed.

Thomas looked like he wanted to melt into the ground, but he leaned in and pecked Alex's lips before swigging from his beer bottle again.

"Oh, that was boring," Noah groaned.

"If you wanna show us how it's done..." Alex shot back with a grin, his arm around Thomas's shoulders.

Noah grabbed Cam and bent him backward – even though they were seated side-by-side at the picnic table – for a kiss.

Cam nearly spilled his beer, flailing to grab Noah for balance as Noah kissed him deeply.

Even their parents were laughing at Cam being utterly caught off-guard, his eyes comically huge. Floyd, unlucky enough to share the bench with them, leaned back as far as he could from them and pulled a face while Chase laughed loudly.

Then, Chase stood up beside Jackson and pecked his lips sweetly – a lot less shyly than Thomas had, but not as blatant as Noah. "To all of us," he toasted, pulling Jackson to sit back down again.

Everyone toasted that and drank again.

"And," Cam added, not even bothering standing up, "to Kevin. We're seeing him off in just a couple days."

"Aw, no," Kevin waved his hand. "I don't do goodbye parties."

"To the best *damn* hockey player I know," Cam insisted, leaning over to punch his shoulder. "Coach Walker's gonna have a field day with you unless you practice your crossovers harder."

"Yeah, yeah," Kevin groaned to laughter. Cam hadn't even

acted a bit jealous since hearing that Kevin was due to head to training camp to fill the very same spot he once held.

Instead, he'd pumped Kevin full of advice, even taking him for some one-on-one exercises at the town court. Now that he could exercise again, he'd taken full advantage of that fact.

The Rileys' parents stood up next, Mrs. Riley urging Mr. Riley to say something.

"Your mother and I just wanted to say," he addressed them as they all went quiet and looked at him, listening closely. "We're very proud of you and glad to have you here. Most of all, we're happy to see you happy. May you be happy for a long time to come."

The "Aww"s were mixed with applause and cheering as he sat down again.

"All right, enough. More burgers!" Jackson told them, wrestling himself free of the picnic table bench to head back to the barbecue. "And more beer."

The sun shone down on them, the grass whispered in the wind, and uplifted, joyful voices floated beyond the fences around their shared backyard.

For the moment, everything was just right.

Crunch (The Riley Brothers #4)

"IS IT TOO LATE TO LISTEN?"

Floyd Turner has come through hell to own a tattoo shop downtown. But, as big and tough as he is, the idea of showing up single at his high school reunion makes him nervous. And then his former patrol partner walks in.

Fitness instructor Greyson Peters moved back home, but he's still carrying his scars. He's decided on a tattoo to cover up the physical ones, at least. That'll help him stay confident—and on his own path. And who better than Floyd to help with that?

Both men are struggling to find closure, and it turns out Floyd isn't the only one nervous about the reunion. They could always be fake dates… but how fake is it when these feelings are so terrifyingly real?

Crunch is the fourth book in The Riley Brothers, a low-angst series filled with brotherly banter and small-town smiles. This steamy, standalone gay romance novel can be enjoyed on its own, and promises a happily-ever-after ending.

About the Author

E. Davies writes feel-good, low-angst romance that never fades to black when the going gets good! Born in Canada, after 16 moves and counting, Ed has finally put down roots in north London.

He emerges from his writing nest to coo over fuzzy animals, flee from cute guys, dance through the streets with his chosen family, put together fierce looks, and—most of all —befriend local flowers.

You can find all available titles at: www.edaviesbooks.com

FOLLOW E. DAVIES ONLINE:

amazon.com/author/edavies
bookbub.com/authors/e-davies
facebook.com/edaviesauthor
goodreads.com/edavies
instagram.com/edaviesauthor
x.com/edaviesauthor

Sunrise Island Brothers:

Collide

Stranded

Hart's Bay:

Hard Hart

Changed Hart

Wild Hart

Stolen Hart

Significant Brothers:

Splinter

Grasp

Slick

Trace

Clutch

Tremble

Riley Brothers:

Buzz

Clang

Swish

Crunch

Slam

Grind

Brooklyn Boys:

Electric Sunshine

Live Wire

Boiling Point

F-Word:

Flaunt

Freak

Faux

Forever

Freedom

After:

Afterburn

Afterglow

Aftermath

Shared Universes:

Shelter

Adore

Miracle

Redemption

Limelight

Barely Regal